BOUND

MEN OF CLUB TRISKELION

J.L. QUICK

AUTHOR'S NOTE

This novel is a contemporary dark romance. It contains scenes and descriptive adult content, recommended for adult (18+) readers.

As a contemporary, dark romance work of fiction, this novel is not intended to be a portrayal of a healthy relationship or a 'how to guide' for the kink and lifestyle elements depicted within.

For those interested in exploring aspects of kink and/or dominant-submissive relationships explored in the following chapters, please do so responsibly and with appropriate reference materials.

TRIGGER WARNINGS

This novel may contain scenes and descriptive adult content that might be triggering for some readers.

GLOSSARY

This novel contains dialect commonly found in Ireland and Great Britain.

A stóirín—My little treasure

Arse—Ass

Bloke—Guy/dude

Bloody—Damned/Fucking/Very

Daidi—Daddy

Feek—Someone attractive

Go hifreann leat a shliomadoir lofa—To hell with you, you rotten bastard

Gnéasach—Sexy

Mam—Mom/mother

Mammy—Mommy

Mhamó—Grandmother

Mo Chéadsearc—My first love

Mo ghrá—My Love

Pakhan—Head of the Bratva

Póg mo thóin—Kiss my ass

Rud ar bith do mo dheartháir—Anything for my brother

Rud ar bith do mo theaghlach—Anything for my family

Shite—shit

Tá tú go hálainn—You are beautiful

The FDR – Franklin D. Roosevelt Drive (NYC Highway)

Twat—Obnoxious or stupid person

Uncail—Uncle

To the survivors who braved the storm and came out stronger...

CHAPTER ONE
DECLAN

"You're a fucking twat, Finn."

Muttering under his breath like a child, Finn grumbles, "*Póg mo thóin*. You're a fucking twat."

Maybe I should've let Tristan choke his arse out a few months ago.

"Just grab his bloody feet," I snarl as my eyes dart down the dead man's bruised body in the back of my Suburban. Finn does as he's told—*for once*—and helps me drag the heavy weight down to the waterfront of the Hudson River. With all the rain the past few days, the water is high and the current should be strong enough to drag him into the Atlantic long before he surfaces. With any luck, the fish will have at him before then. Both of us give a lofty swing and toss him into the water. He hits with a splash, and I huff, "How many more strippers do you need to fuck before you finally realize they're nothing but trouble?"

"*This one* wasn't my fault." He tips his head to the dead guy, quickly floating downstream.

Of course not.

Nothing is ever Finnegan's fault.

"The Bratva's accountant? Not your fault, either?"

"Nah, I own that one." He smirks with a hearty chuckle. "It's not my fault this girl didn't exactly say she was seeing anyone. And she sure as fuck didn't let me know that it was his bed I was fucking her in."

"So, we are clear you started a fucking war?" I take a deep breath and try to maintain my composure as I wipe my soiled hands on the front of Finn's T-shirt. "Maybe in the future, to prevent me from having to help you get rid of another body, you find out *if* the girl you are taking home is seeing anyone. And maybe… Just maybe, for added measure, you don't fuck some poor bloke's girl in *his* bed."

"I think he was more upset that she was getting properly dicked than the fact it was in his bed," he laughs. "Pretty sure he's never heard her scream like that before."

"Jesus fucking Christ! You're worse than trying to rationalize with Fiona."

The gravel crunches under our feet as we walk back to the SUV, and Finn abruptly shares, "Seriously though, the whole fucking building can tell you how many times she came."

Tristan shouts as he closes the hatch of the Suburban, "If you two are done, can we get out of here before we get caught tossing bodies into the river? I would like to go home, climb into bed and"—he air quotes with an eye roll—"*properly dick* my wife."

The three of us climb into the SUV and fight bumper-to-bumper traffic as we head back into the city. For most of the ride, I manage to bite my tongue, but when we come to a dead stop a few miles from Finn's apartment, my curiosity gets the better of me. "I know I'm going to regret this," I sigh. "What is the fascination with strippers?"

He leans forward, rests his forearms on the back of my and Tristan's seats and presses himself between them before emphatically responding, "What *isn't* there to be fascinated with? Perky tits, tight bodies, flexible as fuck, and stamina for days."

I'm about to reply when he leans closer and divulges, "And more often than not, they have an ungodly amount of father figure issues they need help resolving. Meaning they'll do just about anything for a little praise and reassurance."

"I'm sorry I fucking asked." I shake my head, relieved when the light finally turns green and we can pull through the intersection.

"You asked, old man." He chuckles, sliding back.

Tristan laughs from the passenger seat, and I can't hide the displeased scowl spreading across my face. "What?"

he laughs. "You *did* fucking ask. Were you really expecting a philosophical discussion or eloquent words of wisdom?"

"All I'm saying is don't knock it until you've tried it," Finn chimes in from the backseat. "We all know you haven't fucked anyone in a long while, and I'm sure Candy would be more than willing—"

"I am *not* fucking the girl you had your cock in an hour ago." I cut him off. Pulling to the curb in front of his apartment building, I huff, "Just get out, and let's pretend I never wanted to know."

"Your loss." He smirks as he climbs from the backseat. "She sucks better than a Hoover."

For fuck's sake.

Merging back into traffic, I can feel Tristan's eyes on me. Turning to face him, I gruffly ask, "What?"

"He makes a valid point."

"You've got to be kidding me?"

"Not about the fucking strippers," Tristan clarifies, solemnly shaking his head. "It's been a while—"

"It's barely been a year, Tris," I bark.

Disposing of a body because of Finnigan's recklessness was not on my agenda for this evening. And I definitely didn't sign up for a heart-to-heart regarding my non-existent sex life. I flex my fingers around the leather of the steering wheel, trying not to explode at Tristan. My knuckles whiten from my tightening grip when he continues to push the matter. "We both know damn well that isn't true."

"The fuck it isn't!" I snap as we pull into the parking garage. Seeing red, I slam on the brakes, throw the Suburban into park, and violently fist the front of Tristan's shirt. "I didn't once break my vows when I was married to her, and I sure as fuck haven't slept with anyone since Sarah."

"Relax." Tristan's tone is soft as he lightly grips my wrist to pull my hands from his shirt. "I'm not implying you were ever unfaithful to her. Quite the opposite, actually. You started mourning her long before she was gone, Dec."

He isn't wrong.

My celibacy began well before Sarah's actual passing, not long after I realized I was literally going to watch her die. Dropping my grip on Tristan and sliding out of the SUV, I share, "I'm not ready. Quite frankly, I don't know if I'll ever be ready."

"None of us are pushing you to get laid. Well, except Finn," Tristan jokes and forces me to crack a small smile. "We just don't want you to spend the rest of your life wondering what if?"

I wish it were that simple.

Memories of our life together aren't the only thing that has kept me from moving on.

"God forbid you ever lose Layla. You'll finally understand, then. And, more than anything, I hope that you never actually understand an ounce of what I've been through."

CHAPTER TWO
QUINN

When I wanted to get together to talk with Layla tonight, I was not expecting her driver to bring me here—Declan's home.

It looks nothing like what I expected or what I had imagined his place would be like. With the clean-cut way he dresses and his gruff demeanor, I expected his place to mimic that—leather, dark wood, and minimalist. Instead, the massive open floor plan is warm and welcoming.

Two things he is not.

My fingers dust over the back of the soft, oatmeal tweed couch. It's an odd design choice for someone with a preschooler, clearly evidenced by the squiggly, bright green trail of marker beneath my fingertips. I round the sofa with my glass of Pinot Noir and take a seat, sinking into the softness of the cushion as I adjust the navy throw pillow beside me. Waiting for Layla to join me with her glass, my gaze roams over the room.

The soft brown walls are adorned with floral art in various muted tones to accent the soft coziness of the space; and black and white family photographs spanning as far back as pictures of the Evans brothers younger than when I first met them. Tucked in the corner not far from the couch is an adorable midnight-blue, Fiona-sized armchair and a small bookshelf packed full of childhood favorites. Other toys are scattered haphazardly around the living area, and Layla gathers a handful of them before dropping them into a small wicker basket as she makes her way to the couch and takes a seat beside me.

Even though I only met Declan's late wife, Sarah, a handful of times before she fell ill, everything about this space reminds me of her. She was always so warm, welcoming, and down to earth.

"I know you don't want it," Layla continues our conversation from the kitchen, "but you know the boys will take care of you."

Swallowing my sip of red wine, I exhale. "I know." The Evans brothers have been footing my bills since that night at the bar, each of them letting me know countless times that there is no expiration for their offers to take care of me. All of them harbor an element of guilt for what happened to me—something that was clearly not their fault. "But you're right. I don't want it. I just can't keep taking their money for nothing."

"It's not for nothing," Layla corrects. "You're family to all of them, and they are merely taking care of someone they love."

I'm not their family...

Her words both warm and break my heart. I've always wanted to be a part of this family, but not like this. I don't want to be the charity case they all feel they *need* to take care of.

It wasn't always like this between us. We were all thick as thieves when we were younger, and for the longest time, the Evans brothers were like my actual brothers. The five of them would do anything to protect me. Other kids. My mother's many boyfriends. No one stood a chance against the boys who had practically adopted me as their sister.

At least until we all went and fucked it up.

"It feels wrong, like I'm taking advantage. I would feel better about it if I were actually earning my keep." Unfortunately, I'm basically useless being hired for any kind of job that would be worthwhile for them. Crowds, loud noises, and sometimes simply being out in public often result in a panic attack. *Sweaty and hyperventilating isn't exactly a good look on me.* "I can't go back to the bar. And while I know it's quieter and has more security, I don't think I'm at a place where I could handle the atmosphere of the club either."

"I get that, Quinn. I really do. But you also know these boys aren't exactly capable of taking 'no' for an answer, right?" Layla slaps her hand over her mouth. "Shit! That was insensitive as fuck. I didn't mean it like that. I'm so sorry."

"You don't need to apologize. I'm not *that* broken." I force a slight smile because I *am* still *that* broken. But Layla is the one person who doesn't walk on eggshells with me, and I'm determined to keep it that way. "I've known them my whole life. They might be assholes at times, but not one of them would ever—"

My thoughts are cut short when the door opening to the apartment startles me, nearly causing me to spill my wine over the light cushion of the couch beneath me. My fingers tighten around the stem of my glass—with enough force that I'm surprised it doesn't snap in my fist —as my heart begins to race. Seeing my distress, Layla leans forward and lightly wraps her hand around mine, clutching the wine stem. "It's okay." Her tone is soft and comforting. "It's just Tris and Declan."

Closing my eyes, I take a deep breath and count backward—*five, four, three, two, one*—unsuccessfully trying to calm myself and slow my speeding heart before I spiral into a full-blown panic attack. Opening my eyes, I suddenly find myself locked with Declan's slightly bewildered gaze from across the room. My sudden panic might be dissipating, but my heart still thumps a little harder.

"Quinn." My name slowly rolls over Declan's lips with his rich, deep tone as he acknowledges my unexpected presence, his deep-blue eyes not once wavering from our locked stare.

"I hope you don't mind." Layla's words draw Declan's attention from me. "She needed to talk, and I knew you guys would be awhile taking care of...um...business."

"Subtle, *mo chuisle*," Tristan chuckles as he slips his fingers under Layla's chin and tips her face toward his before lightly kissing her lips. Standing against the back of the couch, Tristan's hand lingers over Layla's shoulder as he continues, "I've told you; Quinn knows what we do for business."

Removing his black zip-up hoodie, Declan drapes it over the back of the barstool at the island. Crossing his arms over his chest, he leans back against the island. "Quinn is like a sister to all of us. There are no secrets between any of us."

Well, except that one...

...and then the many that stemmed from it.

CHAPTER THREE
DECLAN

"What brought you over here after midnight, anyway?" I inquire, not realizing how abrasive my question sounds until I watch Quinn become visibly more uncomfortable before my eyes. Uncrossing my arms, trying to look less standoffish, I soften. "Is everything okay?"

"No. I mean...not really," she responds softly as she shakes her head. "I can't—"

"*Daidí?*" Fiona's sweet voice cracks through her sleepy grumble as she toddles down the hall and toward me, unintentionally interrupting Quinn. Her hot-pink floral pajamas are wrinkled. Her usually unruly, curly red hair is disheveled, and her eyes are clearly tired.

Bending down, I wrap my arms around her and lift her tiny body from the floor, swallowing her in my embrace. I place a soft kiss against her forehead. "Did we wake you up, *a stóirín?*" I gently ask.

"No," she mutters as her arms wrap tightly around my neck and nuzzles into me. I should take her back to bed. Instead, I pull out the barstool and slide into it with Fiona snuggled against me on my lap to give Quinn the opportunity to finish what she wanted to say.

"You can't what?" I prod Quinn to continue while gently petting Fiona's untamed hair, attempting to get her back to sleep.

"I can't keep taking your money," Quinn blurts as Layla stands from the couch.

"Yes, you can," Tristan responds matter-of-factly before I have time to say a word.

Layla walks around the couch and toward me before turning back toward Quinn and teasingly snarking, "I told you so." Quinn rolls her eyes as she lets out a gentle huff of annoyance in response.

"Funny, Layla. But I'm serious," Quinn exhales. "I can't keep just taking your money. I know you all mean well. Truly, I do, and I've appreciated it these past few months more than I could ever express. But I just can't."

"We're not going to let you wind up homeless and destitute," I retort, knowing that it's only going to ignite her stubbornness.

As expected, she digs in her figurative heels and rebuts, "I'm not going to take your money. I will withdraw every dollar and carry it to the club to return it if I have to, but I cannot continue to accept your money."

Layla tenderly pulls Fiona from my lap and into her arms. "Let me put my sleepy little shortcake back to bed while you three fight over this." Fiona's head lolls on Layla's shoulder as she carries her down the hall and back to her bed. Layla is fantastic with Fiona. It's a shame that the best nanny I've ever had is my brother's wife. I can't exactly expect her to move in and be at my beck and call. But she's what Fiona deserves—someone who will love her like their own.

Tristan takes Layla's seat on the couch beside Quinn and lightly grips her hand. "What happened to you *is* our fault—"

"No. it's not. You all need to stop blaming yourselves. You didn't—"

"We may not have hurt you, but you know as much as the rest of us it never would've happened if it weren't for who we are," Tristan refutes her claim.

Quinn might not blame us, but I've—*we've all*—been riddled with guilt from the first police call on that night at *Deartháir*. She was safer in Ireland. She should've stayed away—far away from us.

From me.

We aren't good for her. We never have been.

And we never will be.

"I will repeat it to the lot of you until I'm blue in the face." Quinn pauses before vehemently insisting, "*You* are not responsible for what happened to me. *I* didn't lock the door. *I* sent Isaac home early, leaving me there alone. *I* didn't dial 911 the moment they came inside after being told the bar was closed. *I* am responsible for what happened to me."

She's always been so fucking strong-willed, and it's fucking infuriating. After sliding from my barstool, I shift my weight as I fight the urge to storm across the room. With my jaw clenched, I loudly assert, "It was *our* bloody bar! Just take the fucking money!"

"I'm not taking your money, Declan," Quinn barks as her cheeks slowly begin to turn a shade of red, similar to that of her hair. "I'm not a charity. I earn my money."

"Shhhh!" Layla whisper-shouts as she storms toward us from the hallway. "The two of you are going to wake Fiona up again. Both of you are so damn stubborn."

I'm not being stubborn. I'm right. I'm just trying to take care of her, like I promised.

"We don't need to fight about this," I dictate, crossing my arms and glaring at Quinn, "because we are not going to stop taking care of you."

"If I'm not working for it, I don't want it," Quinn mimics my tone and mockingly crosses her arms to mirror my stance while raising a brow.

"You are all impossible!" Layla exclaims, tossing her arms in the air. "The solution is pretty simple. Just hire her."

"To do *what?*" Quinn and I reply practically in unison. We all know that she will probably never work in the bar again, and she's been quite clear the club is too much right now, too. Based on how much she jumped when we walked into the apartment, it's not something she will be up to for quite some time.

"She needs a job. You need a nanny. It seems pretty simple to me," Layla states diplomatically, oblivious to what she's actually asking.

"I...I can't," Quinn stammers, her eyes darting between me and Layla. Her lips repeatedly part, and I know she has more to say. *Things we don't talk about.* But no further words come from her. She merely stares at me as though she's waiting for me to fix the Pandora's box that Layla is slowly prying open.

"Why not?" Layla shrugs.

I don't give Quinn a chance to answer and blurt, "She doesn't even like kids." It's a lie. I know it is. I merely said it, hoping she would go along with it. The way her face scrunches, I quickly realize that's not happening.

"I love kids," she huffs.

"Then it's settled," Layla chirps with a pleased smirk spreading across her face. "I'll finish the week with Fiona to give Quinn a chance to get her things in order. She can move in over the weekend."

What the fuck just happened?

CHAPTER FOUR
QUINN

I have cursed Layla nearly every day this week. As I watch the movers grab the last box from the entryway, I swear silently once more about the situation she's put me in.

Not that she is even remotely aware of what she's done.

And not that I plan to tell her.

When I finish, I take a moment to silently berate myself. As much as Layla is the one who insisted I become Fiona's nanny, I'm the one who could have denounced the whole idea. What scares me is that part of me wanted this—because I could have said no. I had almost a week to get out of this.

But I didn't.

And then again, neither did Declan.

"We'll head straight to your new place with your things,

ma'am," the guy in charge of the moving crew explains. "Are you sure you don't want a ride over there?"

"No. Uh...I mean...no, thank you," I fumble through the rejection of his offer. While he seems nice, and I am certain he means well, I'm not getting in the car with a man I don't know. Being alone in this apartment with four strange men was stress-inducing enough. It was made only slightly better by the armed security Tristan sent to make me feel safer. "I actually have a friend waiting for me downstairs."

He nods before responding, "Just didn't want to leave you stranded. We'll start unloading as soon as we get across town."

After giving my keys to the super and collecting my security deposit, which I will be forcing Declan to let me give to him in exchange for paying off the remaining months on my lease, I head out to the front of the building. Waiting for me in a large, black Suburban are two of the security guys who work for the Evans. The guy previously in my apartment is behind the wheel. A big, redheaded guy—*I think his name is Rory*—climbs from the passenger seat and opens the rear door of the Suburban for me. "Do you need to make any stops on the way?" he gruffly asks as I slide across the black leather.

I shake my head to answer, and he shuts the door. The moment he retakes his seat upfront and closes his own door, we begin our drive toward Midtown. As usual, it's silent with the exception of the bustling city traffic around us. For what these men have in muscles and their ability to keep us all safe, they definitely lack in conversation skills. I don't even try to hold small talk with the security guys anymore. I'd be better off talking to the back of the seat.

When we pull up to Declan's building, Rory immediately opens my door. I slide out and stand on the sidewalk and stare up at the massive skyscraper before me. This luxurious apartment building is a far cry from the historic, four-story one in Throggs Neck that I've called home for the past three years. "Miss?" Rory's deep voice startles me, immediately drawing my attention. "It's best if we get you inside and off the street."

While I am provided with very sparse details, I am fully aware that the war between the Evans and the Bratva is still in full swing. The news runs rampant with shootings and building fires. Not a day goes by that the boys aren't always riddled with bruises, bloodied knuckles, and, I'm sure, other wounds I'm not privy to.

I'm also not naïve. The blood of one Bratva man is on my hands, and as hard as they tried, I didn't die that night in the bar like I was supposed to. I am both unfinished business and a walking reason for vengeance. My security detail isn't just for my comfort; it's for my protection. *Eventually, they will come for me.*

Rory follows me into the building and, subsequently, the elevator. He reaches around me and presses the button for Declan's floor. Turning to face him, I sarcastically ask, "You moving in too? Will I at least be getting my own room? Or do you need to stay close enough that we will be sharing that, too?"

"You know I have to make sure you get upstairs," he responds. He stares at me for a moment before imparting, "You do also know this is only going to get worse, right?"

"Worse?" I ask, my voice rising a few octaves in confusion. I am already followed *everywhere*, forbidden from using the subway, have men standing outside my building, and God knows what else. How could it possibly be worse?

Rory pauses briefly, and I can't help but think he is hesitating because he knows he's crossing a line. "Declan has more security on that little girl than the president. You probably didn't notice them because he has asked for discretion, so she doesn't know we're around. There are men on the street, in the lobby, patrolling his floor and the stairwells. Security cameras that cover nearly every inch of his home are monitored twenty-four-seven. A fly couldn't land on her without someone knowing."

The weight of what he's saying hits me like a ton of bricks. "You mean..." I mumble.

"*You* now have all of us following you and watching *every* move you make."

Marvelous...

Apparently, I should have asked a few more questions about this job. I'm about to push Rory for more information when the elevator dings and the doors open to the moderately-sized foyer that Declan shares with one other apartment. The space is currently crowded with piles of boxes filled with my belongings and a few smaller pieces of furniture that I didn't have the movers put in storage.

Declan steps through the open door of his apartment with unusually disheveled hair, wearing nothing but a pair of baggy gray sweatpants strung low around his hips. My eyes rake over him, and I gulp so hard at the sight that I hope it isn't audible. Pushing forty, he still has pronounced pecs and well-chiseled abs. I try to stop myself, but my eyes continue to roam over them to the lines of his Adonis belt, straight to the *very* defined outline at the front of his sweats.

"Are you going to stand there, or are you going to grab a box and let me show around the place?" Declan's gruff voice immediately draws my attention when it has a hint of playfulness to it. I lift my gaze to find his blue eyes staring at me with feigned disapproval and a coy smirk tugging at the corner of his mouth.

Fucking hell...

First day, and he's caught me ogling him. And worse, I think he likes it.

This was a really fucking bad idea.

CHAPTER FIVE
DECLAN

My afternoon was spent forcing Quinn to let me help her stubborn arse unpack her things—or at least move the hundred-pound boxes to her room. Her inability to let anyone help her—*independence, as she calls it*—has always infuriated me. One day of it, I couldn't wait to leave the apartment. This is going to be one hell of an aggravating arrangement.

I should've said no.

I should've fought it.

But fuck if I can figure out why I didn't.

Already needing to get some air, I waited until Fiona was asleep before heading to the club under the ruse of giving Quinn time to get settled on her own. *This, too, was a mistake.* Since arriving, I've already had two women throw themselves at me so violently I'm surprised they didn't break their own necks. It's like they all know my situation and want to be the reason I step back into the lifestyle.

Who knew "fucking the widower" was a kink?

"Whiskey neat?" Jorge asks from behind the bar, and I nod while surveying the room for any of my brothers. I don't find any of them, but it's late. I'd be surprised if they haven't already ventured down the hall to a private room. Jorge returns a moment later with my glass and slides it across the bar. "Wasn't expecting to see you here tonight. Isn't Quinn moving in today?"

"She's my new nanny, Jorge, not my girlfriend." I take a gulp from the glass, the amber liquid burning as it runs down my throat.

"I'm sorry. I just figured with your history—"

"We don't have history," I bark. The sudden look of confusion spreading across his face quickly tells me he was referring to our childhood friendship and not the secret the two of us have been harboring for the past fifteen years.

The phone on my nightstand ringing wakes me, and I roll over to answer it. As I reach for it, I note the time—2:47 a.m.

"What'd you do this time, Finn?" I groggily huff as I pull the phone to my ear.

"Dec?" a soft, pained Irish accent cracks when I answer the phone.

"Quinn?"

"I'm sorry, but can you come get me?" she chokes through a sob. I huff in annoyance, the lot of them always calling when they need me to get them out of trouble. As I sit up in bed, she whispers through the phone, "He wouldn't take no... He tried to..."

"Where are you?" I snarl, immediately seeing red. I toss back the covers and firmly plant my feet on the ground, ready to run to her.

"The bathroom. I locked myse—"

"No, Quinn! Where the fuck are you?" I interrupt her, needing to know how to get to her. Now. She rattles off an address not far from my place as I quickly pull on my pants and shoes. "I'll be there in five."

After abruptly hanging up the phone, I grab a sweatshirt from the floor and pull it on as I head toward the kitchen for my keys. My steps are fast and heavy, echoing off the concrete as I make my way through the parking garage. I cannot get behind the wheel of my Shelby fast enough.

I reach the address Quinn gave me and am surprised to find it's a brownstone with a party in full swing. Drunks stagger down the front steps and into the street as music blares through the open front door. I park half on the sidewalk, and I take the steps two at a time and push through the front door before heading upstairs.

I shove open the first door as I rush down the hall. Empty. Muffled cries come through the second, and I'm about to barrel through it with my shoulder when I hear her broken screams come from down the hall. "Stop! Help! Someone!"

"You don't get to be a fucking tease all night and not be expected to fucking put out," a tall, muscular blond snarls as he pulls Quinn from the bathroom by her hair.

"She said no," I shout over Quinn's screams for help as the blond bends her over the bed and hikes her skirt around her waist.

"Dec..." Quinn pleads for help through the tears streaming from her bloodshot eyes.

He stares at me as he hastily undoes his pants and claws at her panties. "This doesn't fucking concern you, Dick. Get out and shut the fucking door."

"But it does," I mutter under my breath. Turning on my heel, I push the door shut and click the lock.

"Dirty little teases get exactly what they ask for," the blond shoves her face into the mattress before realizing I haven't left the room. "Stay if you want, but there won't be much left of her by the time I'm done."

"I could say the same about you." I snidely reply, seconds before rushing and tackling him to the ground. Quinn curls into a ball on the bed in a pile of tears as I pound at the man pinned beneath the weight of my body. My fists pummel his face until my knuckles are cracked and bleeding like the skin they're crashing into. But I don't stop. I hit him again and again until he no longer resembles a man, not stopping until he is a limp pile of bloody skin and broken bones beneath me.

"You have no idea just how much she concerns me," I whisper, wiping my bloodstained hands across his shirt before climbing

from his dead body. Turning, I find Quinn tucked into a ball, still exposed, and sobbing uncontrollably. I approach her slowly and try to comfort her. "You're safe, Quinn. I'm here."

Hooking my fingers under her panties, I pull them back into place before lowering her skirt and helping her from the bed. Her tears dampen my sweatshirt as she holds on to me tightly and sobs into my chest. As I hold her against me, I place a kiss on the top of her forehead while pushing back thoughts I shouldn't be having about her.

Pulling back slightly, she stares up at me with her big green eyes as she releases the fistfuls of my shirt. Not caring about the blood droplets staining my skin, her fingers lightly rub over my cheek. Her lower lip quivers as her words tremble over it. "Thank you."

"I've got you." I cup her face and stare down at her. "No one will ever hurt you."

CHAPTER SIX
QUINN

Last night was my first full night of sleep in months. No nightmares. No tossing and turning. Not even that normal unease of sleeping somewhere new. I woke up feeling completely refreshed. Which, based on yesterday afternoon, is going to come in quite handy for trying to keep up with the massive amount of energy Fiona has.

Pulling my hair into a messy bun atop my head, I take a quick shower and throw on a pair of yoga shorts and a baggy tank top. After applying a few swipes of mascara, I head down the hall and am surprised to find both Declan and Fiona already awake.

"What do you want for breakfast this morning, *a stóirín?*" Declan croons to Fiona, currently standing atop his bare feet in her Hello Kitty pajamas. Her giggles fill the apartment as he marches her through the kitchen. The sight of the two of them is unbelievably adorable—*and so unlike the Declan I know*—that I pause at the edge of the kitchen merely to watch the two of them.

"Waffles!" Fiona shouts her giggly response, causing a smile to spread across my face.

"Again?" Declan dramatically questions as he dips at the waist to pull Fiona into his arms. Peppering kisses across her face as she laughs even harder, he teases, "You're going to turn into a waffle, *a stóirín.*"

I'm pretty sure my ovaries just fluttered.

Fiona catches a glimpse of me over Declan's shoulder and boldly declares with a broad grin, "Quinn wants waffles too!"

Declan turns at the sound of my name as he places Fiona back on the floor. "Is that so?" He rakes his fingers through his graying morning bedhead as he stands until I'm met with his searing blue eyes and a sheepish smirk. "Is that what you want?"

Yup, they definitely fluttered.

"Y...yeah," I stammer, mentally trying to remind myself he's asking about the waffles.

I haven't had an inkling of a sexual thought—*at least not a positive one*—since the night the Bratva attacked me at the bar. Yet, the second I'm within arm's distance of Declan's rippled abs, my brain turns to mush, and it's the only thing I can seem to think about. This isn't exactly a new problem for me, though. My inability to think about anything else in his presence has plagued me since I was about sixteen.

Declan pulls various ingredients from the cabinets and plugs in the waffle maker. Awkwardly inching toward the counter, I ask, "Do you need any help?"

"Someone," he teasingly eyes Fiona, "has requested waffles every day this month. At this point, I could make them with my eyes closed."

Who is this man?

The Declan Evans I grew up with is egocentric and irritable. That didn't change as he got older. He actually became grumpier and more standoffish. Yet, inside the confines of this apartment—*or at least when it comes to Fiona*—he's the polar opposite.

Turning my attention from his to Fiona, I feign a gasp. "Every day? You really *are* going to turn into a waffle."

She erupts in a fit of giggles before saying, "You're silly. I can't turn into a waffle."

"What do you say, tomorrow, we give your dad a break from making waffles, and we surprise him with some muffins?" I ask, kneeling down to her level.

"Uh-huh!" She vigorously nods with wide, excited eyes. "Boo-berry ones."

"Blueberry it is, kiddo." I outstretch my hand to officially shake on our agreement. She slides her little hand into mine and enthusiastically shakes it. As I stand, Declan mouths the words *thank you* with an expression that would make anyone think I just saved his life.

The three of us spend breakfast making small talk. Fiona, who tells me in graphic detail about all the toys she plans to show me today, leads most of the conversation. After finishing the last bite of her breakfast, with her lips and chin sticky with syrup droplets, she shares her plans for our tea party and how much she wants to go to the park this afternoon.

"That's a big day you have planned for us." I smile at her over my cup of coffee, wondering how I will ever have the energy to keep up with her. "What are we doing at the park? Swings or slides?"

Declan glares at me for a second before gently informing Fiona, "You'll probably be too tired for the park with the big day you have planned." He wipes a little syrup from her face. "You're all sticky. Why don't you go wash your face and get dressed? I've put your clothes out on your bed. I'll come and give you some help if you need it."

Fiona stands from the table and carefully carries her dishes to the counter by the sink as Declan's displeased gaze falls on me. He stays silent until Fiona disappears down the hallway. "We need to discuss some rules." His voice is gruff, trying to hide his anger.

"Rules?"

"Yes, Quinn. Rules. Under no circumstances will you leave this apartment with my daughter without my permission," he grits. "And I would appreciate it if you didn't get her hopes up about things like going to the park."

There's the Declan I know.

"You can't be serious?" I feel my brows involuntarily pinch together in disbelief. "You want me to keep a three-year-old holed up in this apartment day in, day out?" While his place is massive, and there is plenty of room for her to run and expel her energy, that's no way for a kid to grow up.

"You have no idea how fucking serious I am," he huffs. "She is my fucking world, and it's the only way I can ensure no one will ever hurt her."

"Decla—"

"This isn't the time for your stubbornness, Quinn." He interrupts me. "This is not up for debate. If you can't do as I say, this will not work out. I will find some—"

"Slides!" Fiona shouts, returning from her room. Her face is unwashed, but she is dressed. Even if her shirt is on backward. "We can race on the slides."

Feeling Declan's eyes on me, I force a huge smile and reply, "That sounds fun, kiddo," I pause briefly to shoot an annoyed glance at Declan. "Hopefully, we both won't be too tired from all the other fun you have planned for us today."

Declan pushes back his chair and stands from the table. "*Daidi* needs to get ready and head to work." He gives Fiona a kiss on the forehead. "Be a good girl for Quinn today."

"Yes, *daidi*."

"I love you, *a stóirín*." Declan stares at me for a moment after saying goodbye to her, and leaves without another word to me.

CHAPTER SEVEN
DECLAN

The entire drive to the club is spent thinking about Quinn and how fucking stubborn she is. With every block that passes, I find myself growing more concerned that she isn't going to adhere to the single rule I left her with. After pushing the Bluetooth button on the steering wheel, I transcribe a text message to her.

> I was, and am, very serious about not leaving the house, Quinn.

Her response flashes across the screen almost instantly.

QUINN

> Really???

> Because it kind of came across like you were joking and didn't mean it.

My fingers flex around the steering wheel, and I hit the button on the touchscreen to dial her number. I don't give her a chance to speak when she answers the ringing phone, immediately snarling, "Qui—"

"Relax, Dec," She interrupts me with an exasperated sigh. It's so obnoxious that I can practically hear her eyes rolling. "I got it. We won't leave, and I'll guard your little treasure like she's my own. Just know this is something that I want to discuss with you later."

"My rules aren't up for debate," I snip.

"Well, that's good because I said I plan to *discuss* them with you," she retorts, oozing with sass. "Now, if you don't mind, I have a very important princess tea party to return to."

The line goes silent.

Did she really just fucking hang up on me?

I am fuming when I pull into the club. I slide out of the Suburban and slam the door shut, only to be met with a deep, hearty laugh. "Things going that well?" Liam stands by the parked car beside me with an amused smile. He gestures at his car and instructs, "Get in. I could use some help, and you look like you could beat the piss out of someone."

He isn't wrong. For as long as I can remember, Quinn has had a way of getting under my skin, unlike anyone I've ever met.

"Where are we headed?" I inquire as Liam pulls from the lot.

Weaving through the city traffic and heading toward Brighton Beach, he answers, "I got a lead on how to get to the Pakhan."

In the hour it takes him to get to Brooklyn, I repeatedly pull up the security feed on my cell phone to check the cameras. Each time, I find Quinn and Fiona in the apartment, laughing and having fun together.

"You gonna watch that thing all day?" Liam asks, eyeing the livestream on my phone. "It's Quinn. You know you can trust her with Fiona." As much as I hate to admit it, I know he's right. I'm the one who has repeatedly failed her; Quinn has never given me a reason to have any doubt in her.

Liam pulls his Maserati to the curb, which stands out like a sore thumb against the Chevys and Nissans parked along the street. He gestures toward a small coffee shop. "This way." I follow him inside, past the counter, and straight toward a backroom.

The windowless office is dimly lit, the few flickering fluorescent lights flashing over the cheap wood paneling on the walls. A grotesque, portly man with gray hair and an unkept beard sits behind a wooden desk covered in papers. The thick air is full of overwhelming scents, the coffee, cigarette smoke, and baked goods doing nothing to mask the rank body odor of the man before me. Smoke billows from his mouth with every word he speaks. "To what do I owe the pleasure of a visit from not one but two Evans brothers?"

"Cut the shit, Akim," Liam leans in close, and I can't help but wonder if he is holding his breath. "You know why we're here. We want the Pakhan, and rumor has it you will succeed him. It's in your best interest to cooperate."

Stepping closer and leaning over the desk separating us, my stomach churns at his increased scent. "Just tell us what you know—we don't have to make this an uncomfortable situation. Understand?"

Akim's eyes dart between us, and he swallows hard. "I might know things, but I'm going to need some assurances."

"Assurances?" Liam questions.

"I need you to do something for me." He cocks a brow as he takes a long drag of the cigarette hanging from his lip. "Prove to me that you're going to uphold your end of this deal and that you won't double-cross me once you get what you want."

"You've got to be fucking kidding me?" I huff. "You want *us* to work for *you*?" The room falls silent except for Akim's heavy breathing, only further polluting the air flooding my nostrils.

"One of my guys ran off with one of my whores." Akim pauses as he crushes the cigarette butt into an ashtray before pulling a fresh one from the near-empty pack on the desk before him.

"You want us to bring them back?" Liam asks.

"Her. Bring Kira back. Her sweet little cunt hasn't worked off her debt to me yet," a wicked smirk spreads across his face. "Kill Luka. I have no use for disobedient soldiers who think they can fuck my girls for free."

I shoot a glance at Liam, hoping he tells this disgusting slob to go to hell, but he doesn't. "That all?"

"I have one other small ask," he speaks slowly, his accent more pronounced, "but after you bring me back my Kira." Liam nods, and I'm ready to crack him for committing us to this job. "Rumor has it they are hiding out in Chinatown."

Akim slides a photo across the desk until it's before me. On it is a beautiful young blonde. She barely looks old enough to buy herself a beer. Swiping the photo from beneath his hand, I tuck it into the pocket of my jacket without taking a further look at it. Deepening his tone and raising his voice to be heard outside this office shouts, "Now, get out of my office and get the fuck out of Brighton!"

I bite my tongue until we are back in the car, immediately unloading on Liam once the doors are shut. "You can't be serious about working with that fat fucking slob! Or putting him in charge of the Bratva."

"Fuck, no!" Liam spits, gunning the engine. "The minute I get what I want, I'm going to cut his throat and watch smoke billow out of him like a fucking chimney."

CHAPTER EIGHT
QUINN

In the week I've been living here, I've fallen into a routine. Taking care of Fiona is a breeze, but that might be because she is the most even-tempered and happiest kid on the planet. *A stark difference to her father.* He's been an unbearable grump, so I haven't paid much mind to the fact that he has been avoiding me or that the majority of communication between us the past couple of days has been occurring entirely via text messages.

Which I'll take because it's the only time he is actually pleasant to me.

DECLAN

Be home in thirty minutes. Bringing pizza.

Still only like cheese?

A tiny gasp falls over my lips when I read his message. It's been years... Decades, even. And he still remembers how I like my pizza.

Yes. Plain cheese.

Thank you.

Thank *you*.

???

For being so good with Fiona.

Have you been watching me on the cameras?

I wait a minute for a response but don't get one.

Well?

Another unanswered text.

We need to talk about a few things tonight.

No wonder this man can't keep a nanny.

"Hey, kiddo," I interrupt Fiona, who is quietly reading in her little corner of the living room. "Your dad is going to be home with dinner soon. Why don't you put your book away, and we can set the table."

Fiona closes her book and shoves it haphazardly back onto the shelf before following me to the kitchen. I open a few cabinets before remembering which holds the plates and glasses I need and put three of each on the counter. "Can you handle the plates?"

"Uh-huh." Fiona nods and reaches for the small stack.

"How about one at a time there, kiddo?" I stop her, worried that she'll drop them.

As Fiona carries the final plate to the table, the door opens, and Declan walks in with two large pizza boxes. "That's a lot of pizza for three people."

After placing the boxes on the table, Declan flips them both open, displaying the cheese pizza and some monstrosity covered in various meats and vegetables, as he teases, "Some of us have developed palettes beyond those of adorable little three-year-olds." He slides a small cheese slice onto her plate and winks at Fiona.

The three of us eat dinner, and Fiona gives Declan the play-by-play of everything we've done today. It is beyond me how she still has this much energy because I am absolutely exhausted. When we all finish, Declan insists on taking care of bathtime and putting Fiona to bed. While it's not exactly my job, I take it upon myself to put away the leftovers and wash the dirty dishes. I aimlessly wander the apartment and pick up stray toys, having finished with my chores before Declan returns—I need to stay busy while I wait for him.

I'm dropping the last of the stuffed animals into a basket when I hear the soles of his shoes echoing down the hallway. When I walk back into the kitchen, I find him pouring a whiskey neat. He turns with a full glass, and his face quickly tells me he is genuinely surprised to find me waiting on the other side of the island. He cocks a brow and imparts, "You might want to get to bed early.

She's going to be waking you before sunrise for those muffins again."

Taking a seat on the barstool beside me, I cross my arms and rest them on the cream marble. "You might want to pour a second because we are finally going to talk about your rules."

"I've got shit to do, Quinn," he husks, ignoring my request and turning to leave the room.

"Yeah, shit like talking to the woman taking care of your kid. And *about* your kid," I retort, trying to quell my anger over being so quickly dismissed. "I'm not letting this go, Dec."

"Fine," he huffs, sliding the glass across the island and pouring himself a new glass. "Hurry up and complain —so I can tell you no and get to the things I *need* to do."

"You *need* to have this conversation," I huff.

"Fine. Then have it."

"Jesus," I exclaim. "I need to know. Do you use up your daily allowance of niceness you are granted each day on Fiona? Or do you just enjoy being a boorish asshole to everyone else in your life?"

"You aren't the first nanny that wants me to change the rules, Quinn. I've had this conversation more times than I can count, so just get it over with."

My fingers dust around the rim of my glass as I try to

maintain my nerve. "If everyone is saying the same thing to you, maybe you should listen."

"She is *my* kid. I will raise her as I see fit," he snarls.

"Then open your fucking eyes, Declan."

"What the fuck is that supposed to mean?"

"You can't keep her locked in this apartment. Holed up like a prisoner. Hiding the dozens of men you have watching her isn't enough for her to grow up normally. She needs a life with pre-school, friends, the park..."—I throw my hands in the air—"For Christ's sake, let the kid go outside to run and play."

His eyes roam over me with a mix of anger and guilt. "You, more than anyone, know it's not safe. I already can't... I'd never forgive myself if anything happened to her."

"Then use that big-ass terrace," I demand. "Give her what she's asking for."

Declan's gaze focuses on the terrace for a moment before turning back toward me and shaking his head.

"They're the Bratva, Declan, not special forces or trained mercenaries. They aren't putting fucking snipers across the way to take out your family."

"Are you done?" he asks, clearly annoyed and not interested in continuing this conversation.

"No." I shake my head. Taking a large swig of the warm whiskey before me, I pause for a minute as the amber liquid heats my throat. "I might be your employee. I might need to follow your rules, no matter how much I think they're actually hurting her instead of protecting her, but I will not ever be okay with you spying on me."

I stand from my barstool and place the glass in the sink before heading down the hall toward my room, calling, "Now I'm done."

CHAPTER NINE
DECLAN

"You're so fucking infuriating," I shout after her, annoyed with myself that I let her get under my skin.

"Maybe," she quips without missing a step, "but you also know I'm right."

That's probably the part that angers me the most.

Pinching the bridge of my nose, I scrunch my face in frustration and let out a deep sigh when Quinn, as she walks further down the hall, disappears into the darkness. Taking a sip from my glass, I mumble through the woodsy burn, "I'm fucking doing the best I can."

Fiona...

Sarah...

Quinn...

I'm doing my best.

But my best is total shite.

I don't know how to handle any of them correctly. *Mo ghrá,* Sarah. I just want to fulfill my promises to her. To honor her as per the vows I made when I became her husband. That's always been the easy one—grieving her and staying true to her—but even that is becoming more of a challenge.

A stóirín, I'm still figuring that out day by day. That was Sarah. She was the one who had the faith in me to be a great father. If she were here, she'd probably be saying the same things to me as Quinn—*as the barrage of nannies before her*—and I'd listen. Eventually.

And Quinn... Not once in my life have I handled Quinn O'Brien correctly. Not that she makes it easy, but she deserves better. Better from me. But I can't. I can't be nice to her; I can't open that door. As shitty as it is to treat her this way, it isn't fair to either of us for me to let her in. I can't let her be more than she is—my nanny.

I can't do that again...

Sipping my whiskey as I walk through the apartment and onto the terrace, my thoughts wander to the night four years ago. A night that has forever changed who I am as a man and eventually turned me into the boorish asshole Quinn sees me as.

Sitting at the busy bar, I stare into the glass in my hands and mull over the decisions that have led me here. Thirty-four years old, and I have spent the last ten years with fleeting and meaningless women passing through my bed because I'm a fucking idiot. Because I shit all over the one good thing that ever happened to me.

"I'll buy you a drink if you pretend to be my boyfriend for five minutes," a petite redhead whispers as she slides up to the bar beside me.

"I'm not interes—" I sulk as my gaze wanders from my glass to an absolutely stunning pair of ocean-blue eyes that I quickly find myself wanting to drown in. The woman standing before me has sheer desperation written across her face. Yet, she is absolutely breathtaking...and about to walk away from me for nearly turning down her request. Slipping my arm around her waist, I quickly pull her flush to me with enough force that she blows a sputtered breath across my cheek. I tuck a tendril of hair behind her ear and lean closer until our lips aren't more than an inch apart. "Exactly how believable does this need to be?"

"Very," she breathlessly exhales the drawn-out word as her eyes bore through me.

With my left arm still tight around her waist, I keep her pressed to my side as my fingers dust from her ear, along her jaw, and to her chin. Slipping them under it, I tip her face up toward mine and lean in closer. I press my lips to hers, and she melts into the kiss—and into me. Sliding my fingers slowly down the length of her throat as I pull back, I ask, "How am I doing?"

"Yes...I...um...good," she stammers as her cheeks pinken, and I immediately realize that I'm fucking done for.

"You owe me a drink..." I pause, waiting for her name.

"Sarah." She coyly smiles as she stares up at me through her thick lashes.

"I'll take a whiskey neat, Sarah."

That's all it took. One drink because she needed to ward off some creep in a bar that wasn't taking 'not interested' as an answer. One drink that turned into four, and the two of us closing down the bar at the end of the evening. For the first night in years, I was more interested in learning who she was than I was in getting her into my bed. One night that made me a husband and, subsequently, a father. That same night put me on the path to becoming the miserable asshole that Quinn called me out as.

Pacing along the terrace's railing, my eyes wander over the buildings across the street as I think about the life I should've had. Wallowing in my grief—and indulging my self-hate over failing the women in my life—I refill my glass a couple times more than I should. With it only making me feel worse, I pour the remainder of the whiskey in my glass down the drain.

As I make my way down the hall toward my room, I pause at Quinn's doorway. I lift my hand to knock but instead, I merely stare at the door. Pulling my hand back, I bring it forward to knock but silently splay my palm over the panel separating us. 'I'm sorry' doesn't seem sufficient, and I don't know what else to say. Instead, I head to my room and grab my wallet before returning to the kitchen to scribble a note for Quinn.

If nothing else, it's a start.

CHAPTER TEN
QUINN

The apartment is unusually silent as I step into the hall. I crack Fiona's door to find her still sound asleep. The door to Declan's room is open, and I glance inside to find his bed doesn't appear to have been slept in. There isn't a sign of him as I walk around the apartment either, except for a scribbled note, laptop, and a black card left on the otherwise barren kitchen island.

You're right. This is the best I can do for now. I left a few websites up on my computer. Get whatever she wants and pay whatever they ask to have it delivered today. I won't be home in time to put Fiona to bed tonight. Please tell her how much I love her. - Dec

I run my finger over the mouse pad of the laptop to find a website for children's outdoor play furniture. Flipping through the different websites and looking at the different swing sets, I turn over the credit card in my hand and mutter to myself, "It's a start."

It took Fiona nearly an hour to settle on the play castle she liked the best. Ordering it took only minutes, and after paying a ridiculously astronomical fee, they agreed to deliver and install it by lunch. I don't know what exhausted me more today, occupying a very giddy little girl as she waited for the delivery guys to put it together or spending the entire afternoon outside.

Having finally tucked Fiona in and gotten her to sleep, I pour myself a glass of wine and get comfortable on the couch before sending Declan a few photos of Fiona from this afternoon—all of them full of huge smiles and sparkling blue eyes.

Thank you.

DECLAN

Thank you.

Maybe next time you don't need to be so ornery about it.

If he listened—even a little—I wouldn't have to be so damn stubborn.

Doubtful.

Maybe next time you'll listen.

Doubtful.

I chuckle as I read his text and can't help the smile that tugs at my lips.

> It's going to be really late by the time I get home, but we really need to talk.

He says nothing more, but I immediately assume it has more to do with things left unsaid than Fiona. I open a book on my phone to pass the time while I wait for him, but I quickly find my eyelids growing heavy as I lose my ability to comprehend the words before me.

The bell dings as the bar door pushes open, reminding me that I forgot to lock it. "Sorry, guys. We're closed."

"We know." A tall guy with a thick Russian accent smirks as he continues to walk toward me.

"That means no drinks, fellas. And you've got to go."

"No." A guy with slicked-back hair shakes his head before turning and locking the door. "I think we're going to stay awhile."

Buzz-cut stalks toward me with an evil hunger in his eyes that causes the hairs on the back of my neck to stand on end. I walk backward, trying to keep the distance between us as his eyes rake over my body. "It's a shame. You sure are pretty."

His words cause my blood to run cold, even as my heart begins to thump harder against my ribcage. I'm so focused on retreating from him that I completely lose track of the third guy until I back into his chest. His burned-tobacco breath wafts over me when he whispers, "Are you going to scream for us? Because I sure fucking prefer when you bitches fight me."

Shoving away from him, I race behind the bar to grab the phone, but I don't make it before Buzz-cut snakes his arms around me. With my hands and legs scrabbling, I scream as I kick at his shins and try to fight him. His friends laugh as he drags me along the bar, my flailing limbs knocking bottles to the floor. He licks up my neck and snarls as he throws me to the booze-and-glass-covered floor, "Oh, she's a fighter."

He's on me before I can push myself from the wet, sticky floor. His hands pull roughly at my jeans, and I scream until my lungs are empty. It's futile; no one is coming to save me. I claw at the floor, tearing up my palms with broken glass until I manage to wrap my hand around the neck of a broken bottle. Holding it tight, I kick at him as I crawl across the hardwood floor to get away from him. He clings to my pants, pulling them down my legs as I work my way from him.

With my clothes torn from my body, he pounces on me and struggles to spread the thighs I'm clenching tightly together. His fingers dig into my skin with such force that his nails break the skin. Gripping the bottle firmly, I swing hard and jam it into his neck.

He gasps as his warm blood coats my hand and spills down my arm. He falls forward, and it sprays over me, the metallic tang coating my tongue as I continue to scream for help.

The guy with slicked-back hair yells something incoherent in Russian as he pulls the dead guy from my half-naked body. I don't need a translator to know what he said. It's very clear from the look on his face and the anger in his eyes as he leans close and fists the front of my shirt. Using his tight hold on me, he lifts me from the floor and throws me toward the bar. I land on the counter with such force that it knocks the wind from me, and my near-limp body rolls from the edge. The barstool shattering beneath me only intensifies the pain of my fall.

I feel more hands on me, and I try to fight them off, but my vision is hazy and slowly blackening around the edges. My lids begin to fall shut, but they snap open when the sting of a palm fires across my cheek. A rough hand grips my burning skin as a deep Russian voice snarls, "You're going to stay awake. If I have to cut the fucking eyelids from your pretty face, you're going to watch every single fucking thing we do to you."

CHAPTER ELEVEN
DECLAN

Liam and I spent the entire day in Chinatown looking for Akim's girl, Kira. They have either split from the area or have one hell of a hideout, because the only thing either of us has to show for it are stomachs full of dumplings and spring rolls.

I told Quinn I was going to be home late, but there was no valid reason for it. We've been back at the club for a few hours now, the five of us sitting in the lounge and splitting a bottle of whiskey as patrons fill the club.

A bottle I am now wishing we would finish faster.

"You arses take it easy on him," Tristan warns as he stands from the table. "I have to go do some mingling bullshit with new members."

My brothers definitely don't heed Tristan's warning. He has barely stepped out of the lounge before they start asking questions about Quinn. It's innocent enough at first, but it definitely doesn't take them long to start harassing me.

"You mean to tell me that not a *thing* has happened between the two of you?" Conor pushes. "We all see how Quinn looks at you. How she's *always* looked at you."

"Nothing has happened since she moved in with me." I try to hide my annoyance, hoping they all quickly drop this conversation. "Trust me, the only thing happening is the two of us fighting."

"So, a good hate-fuck is in your future," Liam jests as he pours himself a refill, and it doesn't take long for Conor and Finn to join in the laughter and jokes.

"The old man hasn't fucked in so long. There's no way he has the stamina for that." Finn can barely get the words out through his laughter. "You can't three-pump a hate-fuck."

"Fuck off, Finn," I spit, even though I know he isn't entirely wrong. When I do come these days, my focus is on the end goal. Definitely not on longevity. It generally involves jacking off in the shower as fast as possible before Fiona walks in on me. Or since she moved in, Quinn. "The whole lot of you can fuck off."

The conversation shifts from me fucking Quinn to me fucking anyone, and eventually, the lot of them grow tired of razzing me. That, and Liam, Finn, and Connor all become a little more preoccupied with their own options for getting fucked. *Literally.* Over the course of an hour, the three of them each gradually depart from the table to flirt with a woman who has caught their eye. Each of them disappears deeper into the club, either to get fucked or to enjoy watching someone else get fucked. I pour the final shot from the bottle and toss it back before deciding to finally go home instead of sitting alone at this table.

I shoot Quinn a quick message to let her know I'm on my way, but it goes unanswered. It continues to go unanswered as I leisurely walk across the street toward my Suburban. An accident has traffic backed up for blocks, and it takes significantly longer than usual for me to get home. Glancing at the dash as I park, it's well after midnight.

When I step through the front door of the apartment, I am caught off-guard by the soft sounds of pained whimpers. Hastily drawing the gun tucked into the waistband of my pants, I inch further into the apartment. I am about to head down the hallway when I realize that the cries are coming from the living room. Peering through the dark, I can't find the source. The room is empty as I sweep across it with my gun poised and ready to shoot. The soft cries grow louder and more fearful as I approach.

Rounding the couch, I am surprised to find Quinn fast asleep. Her lower lip trembles as she near-inaudibly pleads, "Please. Don't."

A single tear rolls down her cheek, and her face scrunches as I tuck my gun back into my waistband. "Oh, Quinn, I'm so fucking sorry," I whisper as I swipe the pad of my thumb over the soft skin of her cheek to collect the rogue tear.

She startles at my touch, and it isn't until her soft pleas become screams of terror and her arms flail at an invisible assailant that I realize it isn't me she's flinching from. "Stop! No!"

Her hands continue to thrash in the air, repeatedly striking my face and chest. I don't try to stop or restrain her because I deserve every slap that lands on my face and fist pounding into my chest.

I broke my promise...

"Quinn," I whisper, gently trying to rouse her from her nightmare, but it does nothing. Her palm strikes my face again, jerking my face to the side as the sting radiates across my cheek. "I'm sorry. I promised you that no one would ever hurt you. And all I've done is break that promise."

Time and time again.

Continuing to take the brunt of her nightmarish fight, I softly stroke her sweat-matted hair and whisper, "You're safe, Quinn. I'm here." I try to be soft, so as not to scare her further, making my attempts to wake her futile.

My face and chest grow tender as she continues to struggle against the assailant in her nightmare, but I don't stop speaking softly to her, "Wake up, Quinn. You're safe. I'm here."

I'll protect you.

CHAPTER TWELVE
QUINN

My own screams startle me awake, and I sit bolt upright in a panic. Cold sweat trickles down my forehead, and my heart pounds painfully hard against my ribcage as I try desperately to catch my breath.

"You're safe, Quinn. I'm here." Declan's soft words both startle and comfort me.

Fisting the front of his shirt, I pull myself into him and sob uncontrollably into his chest. His arms wrap around me, and he pulls me tighter to him. "It's okay. You're okay," he comforts, his hands tenderly caressing my back. As much as I want to push him away, I let him continue to reassure me.

I need it.

His shirt balled tightly in my fists; I pull back enough to see him. Clinging to him and staring up his chest into those deep-blue eyes, it feels like we're back in the bedroom of that frat party—back to that fateful night fifteen years ago.

Declan's face is splattered with the blood of the dead man at our feet. The man he just killed to protect me. Releasing my tight hold on his shirt, I rub my hand over his cheek to wipe it clean. "Thank you," my voice cracks.

"We need to get out of here." Declan's hands slide down my arms until his fingers lace with mine. Without saying another word, he tightens his grip on my hand and drags me behind him. He pulls me through the party to his car, parked half on the curb, before shoving me into the passenger seat. After he pulls away from the sidewalk, he pounds his fists against the steering wheel. "Fuck!"

We drive in silence for a few blocks, which I break when he pulls into the garage nearest his apartment building. "Dec?"

"I can't take you home like that, Quinn." He gestures to my shirt, which I had not noticed was torn. Few words are exchanged as he leads me upstairs and to the master bathroom of his apartment. "You can clean up while I find you something to change into."

I am taken aback when I catch a glimpse of myself in the mirror. Trails of mascara stain my cheeks, one of which is red and swollen from the back of a palm it took earlier tonight. I grab the hand towel from beside the sink, wet it, and begin cleaning the makeup from my face.

Knuckles rap on the open door, and I turn to find Declan holding a neatly folded shirt and a pair of sweatpants. "These are going to be way too big for you, but it's all I have."

"Thank you." I take the clothes from him. He turns to leave me to change in private, and I sputter, "D..Dec. I'm sorry."

Turning on his heel, Declan quickly closes the distance between us. He firmly cups my face in his hands and tilts my face up toward his. His blue eyes bore through me as he stares down at me. "You have nothing to be sorry for."

"You...you killed him...for me."

His voice and eyes are pained as he presses his forehead to mine and shares, "I'd do anything to protect you, Quinn. To keep you safe."

I shake my head as I listen to him. Declan is the first boy I ever had a crush on. I've been in love with him for years. He's made it clear time and time again that he doesn't return the sentiment. "You hate me," I slowly exhale the words.

"I don't hate you." He shakes his head, and his breath wisps over my lips. "I hate having you this close to me. I hate that Conor is fucking infatuated with you. I hate that even though I'm too old for you, I'm also not good enough for you. And most of all, I hate that I can't do the one thing I really want. The one thing I can't fucking stop thinking about."

My breath hitches so hard that I struggle to draw in my next breath. Gazing up at him, my lip quivers as I struggle to find the courage to ask, "What is that?"

"This." His lips vibrate as they crash against mine, setting my body on fire. There is nothing soft or tender about our kiss. It is messy, passionate and full of the need we have both been

harboring. He doesn't just kiss me. He claims me until I am breathlessly whimpering into his mouth.

Without breaking our kiss, he grips the back of my thighs. His fingers dimple into my flesh as he pulls me around his waist. He carries me through the room until I'm pinned to the wall beside his bed. Holding me to it with his body, the hard length in his pants grinds against my panties as his lips and tongue travel along the length of my neck. His lips press to my ear, and I can feel him fumbling with his pants as he groans, "You have no idea how long I've dreamed about this."

"Dec?" I breathlessly moan as he pulls at my panties and aligns himself beneath me. "Wait."

"What?" He pauses. "Are you not on the pill?"

"No," I shake my head. "I'm not."

Declan pulls me from the wall and places me at the edge of the bed before digging into the nightstand and pulling out a condom. Placing the foil wrapper between his teeth, he tears it open and rolls it over himself with obvious experience.

"I'm not the pill because I've never had sex," I blurt as I shamefully cover my face with my hands.

"Quinn," Declan barks, climbing over me and pulling my hands from my face. "You don't need to be embarrassed. And you don't need to do anything you don't want to. I've waited a long time for this. I can wait a little while longer if that's what you need."

I tentatively grip the back of his shirt with my hands and slowly pull it over his head. A slight smile tugs at the corner of his lips as he stares down at me and asks, "Are you sure?"

I nod as Declan dips his head and presses his lips to mine. Unlike before, this kiss is soft and tender as he explores my mouth. "Tell me what you want,"—he languidly kisses the words down my stomach and along my thighs before he removes my skirt and panties—"and I'll give it to you. I'd give you everything, mo chéadsearc."

CHAPTER THIRTEEN
DECLAN

"You're okay." I continue to brush the sweaty hair from her forehead with my eyes locked on hers. Fixated on the gold flecks nestled in the deep emerald of her eyes, I suddenly feel like the stupid twenty-five-year-old kid who would do anything for her again.

I wipe my thumb over a trickling tear, and she shudders when it slides over the still-fresh, small scar running along her cheekbone. "Don't." She sobs when I tenderly drag my finger along it. "It's a reminder every time I look in the mirror of how weak I am."

"Nonsense. It's a reminder of how fucking strong you are. Of how determined you are to live." I continue to trace my finger along the jagged line. Closing what little distance there is between the two of us, I taste the saltiness of her tears on my lips when I place a soft kiss atop the scar and another on her cheek. My lips a breath from her skin, I promise, "You're safe now. I *will* protect you this time."

"Dec?" Quinn tips her head, dragging my lips along her salty cheek until they are resting beside her mouth. Her breaths grow increasingly fast, and she breathlessly whispers, "Tell me why I shouldn't do the one thing I want."

"What do you want?" My lips vibrate against hers as I fight the urge to give in to the one thing I haven't been able to stop thinking about since she was thrust back into my life.

Quinn draws a deep breath and holds it for a second. Her lips part, and her warm breath blows over my lips, "Y—"

"*Daidi!*" Fiona's scared voice carries from down the hall, immediately dissipating the needy tension in the air.

The warmth of Quinn's expelling breath disappears from my lips as her hands fall from their tight hold of my shirt. She barely glances at me as she climbs from the couch and retreats into the cool night air on the terrace. I want to follow her, but the moment is gone. Standing from the couch, I shout, "I'm coming, *a stóirín.*"

With Quinn's screams having woken her, it takes a bit to comfort her and convince her that everything is okay. At least twenty minutes pass before I manage to get her back to sleep. By the time I make my way back into the living room, Quinn is no longer standing on the terrace. Since no one alerted me that she left the apartment, I can only assume she went to bed.

I decide to follow suit. Stripping from my clothes and sliding into bed, I am wide awake when my head hits the pillow.

The more I try not to think about Quinn and our fleeting moment on the couch, the more she infiltrates every last nook and cranny of my thoughts. Flooded with memories of things I've tried so hard to forget, my cock grows hard.

As much as I've tried to ignore it, I yearn to feel the softness of her skin beneath my fingers and enjoy the taste of her on my tongue again. My hand descends beneath the sheets, and I close my eyes and wrap my hand around my cock, giving myself both.

Running my tongue along the length of her inner thigh, I teasingly lick from her knee to the subtle dimple beside her pussy. I nip at the tender flesh of her upper thigh, and her thighs tremble, fighting against the double spiral futomomo.

"You look so fucking good, spread wide and dripping in anticipation of my touch." I kiss the words against her soft, well-groomed cunt. I take a deep breath and inhale the scent of her as my tongue drags teasingly up one plump lip of her cunt and down the other as I fight my urge to bury my face in her.

Sliding my fingers between the ropes binding her thighs to her calves, I pull her against my face as I firmly swirl my tongue around her entrance and up to her clit. She groans with pleasure and need as the swirl of my tongue quickly brings her to the edge. Holding her at the brink, I slip a finger into her. Easing it in and out of her at a brutally slow pace, I command, "Tell me what you want."

I imagine feasting on her, the fantasy so vivid I can practically taste the sweet tang of her. My hand slides languidly over my length, wanting to savor every moment of my fantasy instead of merely providing myself relief.

"Please," she begs, trying futilely to grind her hips against my face. "Make me come."

Thrusting and curling my finger, I grind the flat of my tongue over her clit until she's riding a euphoric wave beneath me. Adding a finger, I thrust hard and deep as I kiss up her stomach. My lips crash against hers, and she rides my hand, moaning as I massage the taste of her onto her tongue.

Her tight cunt quivers around my slick fingers, and I know she's at the edge again. She groans through her bliss, "I need you inside me."

"I am inside you," I tease, adding a third digit and vigorously finger fucking her until her toes are curling and her thighs are trembling in their bindings. Keeping the brutal pace, I grind my fingers into the soft spot of her walls. A gush of warm liquid floods over my hand when she lets go.

I bite my lower lip, the image of her squirting all over me causing my balls to tighten. Stilling my hand and panting, I painfully edge myself because I need more.

Holding the base of my cock, I rub the thick tip through the glistening liquid covering her thighs and pussy. I mercilessly rub it against her clit. "What do you want?"

She arches her back, desperately trying to work me toward her entrance. "Your cock. I need it," she whines so beautifully that I'm unable to deny her. I press into her soaked cunt with ease, causing us both to groan in pleasure. Hooking my fingers under the strands of jute around her waist, I drag her over my rigid shaft as I repeatedly plow into her.

Fervently fisting my length, I imagine her screaming name. I spill over my fist with a guttural moan. "Fuck, Quinn..."

Pulling tissues from the box on my nightstand, I clean my release off my stomach and shamefully shake my head.

I shouldn't do this...

I can't.

CHAPTER FOURTEEN
QUINN

As I slide from bed this morning, I dread stepping from this room to deal with the awkwardness that is awaiting me on the other side.

We've held our secret for fifteen years because it would've destroyed our relationships with his brothers. I've buried my feelings for him and put myself back together too many times because of Declan Evans. A little over a week under the same roof, and *we* nearly let him do it again.

Fuck, I basically asked for it.

When I came back to the States three years ago, I slipped right back into my old life. The Evans brothers took me back in without question. We fell seamlessly into our old rhythms like our friendships were simply put on pause for the decade and a half I spent in Ireland. It was like I never left.

Almost.

The Evans were all exactly the same, just older and a hell of a lot better looking than when I left. Beards, muscles, tattoos, and even a tinge of gray at some of their temples. Each of them still chasing women and getting into fights like they were when I left them—all except Declan.

The real reason I returned to New York.

It was a ridiculous notion, flying across the pond for him. He was my first–crush, love, and partner. What we had wasn't healthy because any relationship you have to hide from the people you love does not end well. Twenty years, and there are still only two people in this world who know what happened between the two of us.

Three, if you count my late mhamó who probably would've kicked my ass before letting me board a plane for him.

Yet, for twenty years, the boy I lusted over at fifteen and gave my body and soul to at nineteen has repeatedly been the man no other could live up to. They might've treated me better and not hid me from the world, but none of them ever made me feel a fraction of what I felt when I was with Declan.

If nothing else, I figured I owed it to myself to see if I was living with some ridiculous memory of puppy-love or if what I felt for him was real. *The moment I saw him, I knew.* It wasn't the gorgeous woman nuzzled against him that broke me; I'd already survived more fleeting women in his life than I could count. It was the look of absolute contentment on his face as his ring-adorned finger dusted over the chubby cheeks of the newborn in his arms. Seeing him the happiest I ever have—*with the things I wanted with him*—nearly destroyed me.

That should've been enough; I should've left. I should've gone back to Ireland and returned to the life I had built for myself. But I didn't. Instead, I stayed and tortured myself with some warped version of exposure therapy. If I proved to myself, day in and day out, that there was no chance with him, eventually, my heart would have to heal. I'd have to get over him. *And I did.* Or at least I managed to convince myself that I didn't care, a notion that went completely out the window last night.

When I step out of my room, finding Declan sitting alone at the island fills me with anxiety. Walking into the kitchen, I avoid making eye contact with him as I pour myself a cup of coffee. With my back to him, I mutter, "We need to talk about last night."

He is silent, and I find him taking a sip from his cup when I turn to face him. The room is so quiet that the light clacking sound it makes against the marble countertop when he sets it down sounds like a sonic boom. "Yes. We do."

Leaning over the opposing side of the island, I fidget nervously with my cup as I struggle to look at him. If I fall into those deep-blue pools of his, I'll never make it through this. We both speak at the same time, resulting in a mash of his "I'm sorry" mixed with my "Thank you."

"You go," he softly instructs.

"Thank you," I muster. Taking a deep breath, I vomit the rest before losing my nerve. "For last night. You really didn't have to, but I appreciate you comforting me. It's been a while since I felt safe like that."

He opens his mouth to speak, but I hold up my hand to stop him. "Please let me finish," I lightly plead, trying to hide the anguish in my tone. Staying silent, he nods and grants me what I'm asking for.

"The way it made me feel was overwhelming, and at the height of all my emotions, I wasn't really thinking. Groggy and afraid, for a moment, I wanted to feel safe with you again. What happened... Or what almost happened between us... It was a mistake," I lie because it wasn't. In that moment, I wanted nothing more than to feel his lips on mine. Had it not been for Fiona's perfectly timed interruption, I would have. I would've torn the lid off the box that I've neatly packed full of all my feelings for him. I would've unraveled my heartstrings and let him in again. I would've let him shatter me all over again to have a second of him on my lips.

I would've, but I'm not going to.

"I shouldn't have, and I'm sorry," I apologize again. Declan's fingers flex around the coffee cup nestled between his palms as he stares at me with a stoic, indiscernible expression. "What were you going to say?"

"That I'm sorry." His tone is just as flat as his expression. "I'm sorry for overstepping. You're my employee, and I crossed a line I shouldn't have."

As much as I'm ending this before it has a chance to get started, his words slice through me in a way that only he has the ability to do. I blink and take a breath, trying to hold back the tears starting to well in my eyes.

"Good?" he asks, sliding from his barstool. I nod, terrified that my voice will break and the dam holding back my tears will immediately follow. "Okay. Fiona is still sleeping. I've got to get to work."

The door clicks shut behind him and I wish it were as simple to close the figurative box we opened. But that lid is tattered and torn.

Not too different from the current status of my heart.

CHAPTER FIFTEEN
DECLAN

It didn't feel like a fucking mistake...

Standing in the foyer, waiting for the elevator to take me down to the lobby, I fight the urge to storm back into the apartment. I want to pull her into me and taste her pouty pink lips—like I should've last night—proving to her that absolutely nothing about what nearly happened between the two of us was a mistake.

I'm not sorry about last night. Not in the slightest. That isn't the apology I was ready to share. The apology I wanted to give was the one that is years overdue. The one I should've been a fucking man about fifteen years ago. *Fuck, if I were a man, I would've done it three years ago.* I would've owned up to how shitty I treated her the moment she reappeared in my life, but I couldn't.

A small part of me was terrified to open up to her and actually let her back into my life. To admit to her everything that happened back then. I was terrified that if I gave her even the smallest piece of my heart the love it held for Sarah would spill out into the void. And I loved Sarah too much to risk that. To risk losing her and the beautiful family we were building together.

God is a cruel fuck, though, because in the end, I lost her anyway.

Probably divine fucking retribution for the shitty life of sin I've led.

And now I've lost Quinn, too.

I've waited far too long, and now it's too late. She gave in to a brief moment of temptation, but that's all it was. A brief moment. *It was a mistake.* She was resoundingly clear this morning.

My phone buzzes as I step into the cab of the elevator. After pulling it from the breast pocket of my jacket, I swipe open the message from Liam.

LIAM

I'll be out front in 5

I'll be down in 2

Finn found Luka and Kira

He's waiting for us in Brighton

Brighton?

Akim is apparently as useless as he looks. They were hiding right under his nose.

My demeanor is apparently as off-putting as my current disposition. For as chatty as he normally is, Liam hasn't once tried to strike up a conversation beyond greeting me when I slid into the passenger seat of his Tahoe.

We pull to a stop in front of a long-forgotten industrial warehouse. Based on its condition and the few people loitering outside of it, it's full of squatters. People don't give a second glance at the addicts and homeless who live in places like this, making it a great place to hide.

"You're keeping some friends in some mighty low places if you managed to find them here," Liam goads Finn.

"Those strippers you lot give me shite about have benefits beyond their perky tits and warm cunts," he quips. "Some of the girls at the clubs have some serious demons. It just took my girls asking around a little to find someone who had seen something."

"You've got *girls* in Brighton Beach?" I inquire.

Finn laughs. "I've got girls all over the city, old man."

As usual, I'm immediately sorry I asked.

The three of us head inside, and the overwhelming stench of body odor, piss, and death floods my nostrils. It's so rank that I don't think anyone will even notice when we leave a body behind.

Liam spots them first and silently alerts us. They're on a dilapidated loveseat in the middle of the room that is soiled with filth. Both of them are asleep. Luka is wedged in the corner, and Kira is curled up beside him with her head resting on his thigh.

Rounding the room, I approach from behind as Liam and Finn walk directly toward them. I flex my hand around the handle of the blade in my hand and silently wedge it against Luka's throat as Liam announces, "Someone has been looking for the two of you."

Startled awake, Luka reaches for the gun, which is resting by his thigh. I pull the blade tighter against his throat, causing it to dimple the skin, and he immediately stills. "We don't want any trouble." His voice cracks with fear as he pulls Kira tighter to him. "We're leaving the city tomorrow."

"Unfortunately, Akim isn't taking very kindly to the two of you running off together," Liam imparts.

Tears well in Kira's eyes as she looks to Luka for help. His voice is gruff as he tries to assert himself, "We aren't going back."

"You're right." Finn grabs Kira's arm and pulls her from Luka. She briefly cries out but doesn't scream like I expect her to.

The shit I will do to protect my family…

"*You* aren't going back." I pull the blade across his throat, severing him from ear to ear. It looks brutal as blood pours down his chest, but by severing both his windpipe and jugular, death should come for him quickly.

Kira is stoic as Finn pulls her through the warehouse and to the Tahoe we left parked at the curb. Shoving her into the backseat, she speaks for the first time. She repeats the same phrase in Russian.

Not understanding her, and knowing my brothers don't either, I try to comfort her. "We aren't going to hurt you." Unlike the Bratva, we don't fuck with women. Selling them, hurting them, and killing them are some of the few things that even our skewed moral compasses aren't okay with.

"Akim will." Her accent is so thick that I barely understand her.

I glare at Liam, and he huffs, "Don't."

As though she knows how much it will affect me, Kira stares at me with huge brown eyes when she shares, "He'll make an example out of me. Show the other girls what happens when you run."

CHAPTER SIXTEEN
DECLAN

"Let it go." Liam shakes his head. "What happens to her isn't our problem."

"You've got to be fucking kidding," I scoff. "When she gets beaten within an inch of her life because we brought her back, that is very much our problem."

Pulling to a stop before Akim's coffee shop, Liam barks at Finn, "Get her out of the car and bring her inside."

"Please," she begs, grabbing my shirt as Finn pulls hers from the SUV. "He'll kil—"

Her words are cut short, muffled by the glass, as Finn slams the door shut.

"Of all days," I huff.

"Fuck. I'm sorry," Liam grabs my arm as I reach for the door handle. "I need her to be believable. She couldn't know. The minute I get what we need from Akim, I'm getting her out of here."

"*Go hifreann leat a shliomadoir lofa!*" I snarl as I climb out of the Tahoe. "I could beat the ever-loving piss out of you."

Liam heads inside, and I stand on the sidewalk for a second, trying to harness my anger before going inside and doing something fucking foolish. After taking a few deep breaths, I open the door and head toward the office we previously visited. I walk through the door just in time to watch Akim's fat fucking mitt crashing into Kira's face. The sound of his fist colliding with her skin echoes off the cheap paneling as she crumples to her knees.

"Whores on their knees are only good for one thing," he spits at her. "Either suck my fucking cock or get the fuck up."

Blood trickles from a small cut beneath her eye, but she manages to hold back the tears welling in her eyes. *This isn't her first round with him, or men like him.* Gulping hard, she reaches for the desk and uses it to pull herself back to her feet.

Akim retakes his seat behind the desk before roughly grabbing Kira's wrist. She winces in pain as he pulls her onto his lap and flush to his sweaty gut. She fights back her disgust—but not the hatred in her eyes toward us— as his hands rub over her skin.

"We held up our end," Liam interrupts Akim's whispers in Kira's ear. "Luka is dead, and you have her back. Tell us what we need to know about the Pakhan."

Kira shivers with what I can only imagine is disgust as Akim licks up the side of her neck, and he chuckles with an evil smirk. "No, you haven't. You seem to be forgetting about something."

"Your small ask?" Liam questions. "What is it?"

The evil smirk on Akim's face spreads into a devilish smile that would make the Cheshire Cat look inviting. "The girl from the bar. The pretty little redheaded one."

My hands involuntarily ball into fists at my sides, and the heat of my boiling blood turns my face red. "That's not a small ask," I push out the words through my gritted teeth.

"She's a fucking barmaid," he grumbles.

"Why her?" I can't stop myself from asking, even though I know the answer.

"What the fuck do you care?" he snarls. Reaching between Kira's thighs, he rubs his palm over her pants before firmly cupping her crotch. "I'm going to tire of this tight little cunt by the time I finish fucking some sense into her. And even if I don't, she'll be fucking useless to me by the time she's done being reminded that she's my whore. My whores do as they're told, and my men will reteach her that as they all get to take a turn."

A single tear rolls down Kira's cheek as she listens to Akim's plans for her. These men—if you can even call them that—are fucking savages.

"When I don't have my sweet little Kira to play with anymore..." Akim's voice trails off as he wipes the tear from Kira's cheek. "Well, I'm going to need a pretty new plaything."

My nostrils flare, and every muscle in my body vibrates with rage. It's as though he knows he's baiting me. I can feel Liam and Finn's eyes on me, willing me to contain myself.

"Besides, I have it on good authority that she's a fantastic fuck." Akim pauses for a moment as his evil gaze meets my heated one. "But she lives with you, so you probably know that already. Don't you? How sweet is her tight little, red-haired cunt?"

Unable to control my anger any longer, I throw myself over his desk, taking him and Kira to the floor. She scrambles from the ground, Liam quickly swooping in to pull her to safety.

"You will *never* fucking lay a hand on her." I climb over the disgusting fucking Russian and pin him to the ground beneath me. My fists crash into his face with unrelenting fury. The barrage of hits causes his spittle and blood to spray over me. His skin splits, and the bones beneath it begin to splinter and break. He gurgles on his own blood—slowly suffocating—as my fists continue to liquefy his face.

By the time I climb from his dead body, I am covered in him. He is unrecognizable, yet he looks exactly like every other man who dared to lay a hand on Quinn.

I made a promise to her, and I will not break it again.

Pushing past Liam and Finn, I'm met with gasps and wide eyes as I walk through the coffee shop and to the SUV out front. My brothers aren't far behind and climb into the Tahoe a few minutes after I slam my door. Neither of them says a word as we drive back to Midtown. A block from my building, I send a text to Quinn.

CHAPTER SEVENTEEN
QUINN

My text goes unanswered, and knowing how bad it can get, I immediately assume the worst. Dropping my phone on the counter, I quickly head down the hall and silently pull Fiona's bedroom door shut.

When I step back into the living room, I'm met with a sight that takes my breath away. Declan. Like I've seen him too many times before. Only this time, it's different, and it chills me to the bone.

Declan stands across the room from me, covered in blood. It's splattered across his face and has nearly saturated his shirt with a deep coating of crimson. The knuckles on both of his hands are split. The cuts have coagulated and his fingers are crusted over with the deep reddish-brown of dried blood as he made his way home.

It isn't the blood that scares me. I've seen him covered in blood and on the brink of death before. It's the complete lack of warmth behind his eyes that has me on edge. They're cold, completely devoid of emotion. It's like his soul has died but his body is here.

"Jesus, Dec!" I exclaim, rushing toward him and feeling over his bloodied clothes for wounds. "Are you okay?"

He stares at me as he shakes his head, but it feels like he's looking through me instead of at me. "No."

"Are you hurt?"

Ignoring my question—and me—he walks to the kitchen and pours himself a drink. His bloody fingers clutching the glass as he pours it down his throat in a single gulp.

"Damn it, Declan. Talk to me."

As though I'm not yelling for his attention, he pours himself a refill, muttering, "You're not my wife. Stop acting like you care."

"Fuck you!" I spit as my palm flies across his cheek before I even realize I've lifted my hand. Tears well in my eyes, and I fight to speak through sobs. "You don't need to remind me that I wasn't enough. You drove that point home fifteen years ago and again when you gave the life I wanted to someone else. But fuck you, Declan, for having the audacity to tell me I don't care about you when you know damn well I've spent my whole fucking life in love with you."

"Fuck, that's not what I meant," he insists.

"It's sure as fuck what you said, though. Clean yourself up before *your* daughter wakes up. *She* doesn't need to know what kind of man you really are." I storm from the kitchen and into my room. I close the door, and I crumple to the floor before falling apart, hating that I let him do this to me again and wondering why I didn't let go after the first time.

My bags are packed. I'm heading to Ireland in the morning to visit Mhamó and tour Trinity College in Dublin before officially accepting my scholarship there. This is the first time I'm not looking forward to this trip. At least, not as much as I usually do. I don't know how I'm going to make it that long without seeing Declan—because we haven't spent a day apart in six months. He's going to use the time that I'm away to break our secret to his brothers, since they are all somehow still oblivious to our relationship. And then, in the fall, he's going to return to Dublin with me.

I wanted to spend the night alone with him. A chance to talk and say goodbye, but Conor, Liam, and Tristan were all adamant they were going to throw me a going away party. Considering I'm only going to be gone a few weeks, I'm pretty sure it was just an excuse to have a party. It's already in full swing when Liam pulls to a stop out front. When I walk toward the front door, I'm surprised to find Declan sitting on the front stoop instead of inside.

"Let me borrow Quinn for a minute so I can say goodbye," He lightly grips my wrist and pulls me from his brothers as we walk up the steps. I take a seat beside him as the boys head inside.

"Bold move, Dec." I tease, but he doesn't crack the slightest hint of a smile, and I immediately realize something is wrong. "What's going on?"

"I'm not going to tell him." He shakes his head.

"Fine." I squeeze his hand. "We'll tell Conor together. He'll understand."

Declan slides my hand from his and places it on my thigh. "He won't. You don't know him like I do."

"What are you saying?"My tone is laced with hurt and confusion.

"I'm not going to ruin my relationship with my brother over you. He's my family. You're just some girl I'm sleeping with."

"You don't mean that." I shake my head. "You love me. You're moving to Ireland with me so we can start a new life. One that won't end with you in prison or getting shot again."

"Do you really think that's true?" His words are cold and heartless. "Do you think that I'm going to leave my family behind? Or that if I really cared for you, I would've hidden you from the most important people in my life?"

"Declan!" I shout his name, tears streaming down my face, as he stands.

Favoring the relatively fresh wound above his hip as he traverses the stairs, he groans, "I'm not going to lose my family over a stupid mistake."

I never saw the inside of my going away party, and I never said goodbye to anyone. I just gave Declan exactly what he wanted. I erased his "stupid mistake" and made myself disappear.

CHAPTER EIGHTEEN
DECLAN

I'm a fucking asshole...

Even for me, this time I went too far.

Giving Quinn well-deserved time to cool off, I took a shower while Fiona was asleep. Then, I bribed Layla to come take her to their place for the night under the guise that neither me nor Quinn were feeling well. I needed to find a way that the two of us could be alone. So we can finally get all our shit out in the open.

Hopefully without killing each other in the process.

"Quinn." I lightly rap my knuckles against her door.

"Fuck off, Declan." Quinn shouts, her anger crystal-clear.

Considering that's the least that I deserve, I'll take it.

"I just need to say one thing. One thing I should've said a long time ago, and then I'll leave you alone."

"At this point, I highly doubt you have anything I'm actually interested in hearing," she snidely responds and I sincerely hope she's wrong.

Standing in the hallway with a door separating us isn't how I wanted to finally say this, but I've left myself no other choice. I fucked it up when I came home. "I lied. I'm so fucking sorry that I lied to you. I should've shouted from the rooftops that I loved you. You were enough, Quinn. You've always been enough, *mo chéadsearc. I* wasn't enough for you."

While I can hear her soft sobs on the other side of the door, she doesn't say a word.

"My brothers needed me after my father died. I pushed you away because I couldn't leave my family, and I knew you would give up your entire life for me. And that fucking terrified me. I would have hated myself for all of my eternal damnation when this life took me from you and left you a widow. I could send you away, or so I thought. I made it six months before I folded. Six anguishing months before I flew across the pond to drag you home with me where you belonged."

"Dec..." Her voice cracks just beyond the panel of wood separating us.

"When I found you at a pub by campus, you were surrounded by your friends. There was a light in you, like nothing I had ever seen. You were happy... So fucking happy. I couldn't bring myself to take that from you. It wouldn't have been right to drown your light and cloak you in my darkness. So I did the first selfless thing in my entire life. What I thought was the right thing. I walked away."

"You selfish fucking prick." Quinn pulls open the door with tears cascading down her cheeks. "That wasn't your choice to make. I was miserable and fucking hated you for years. Part of me still fucking hates you."

"I wanted you to have a better life than the one I could give you."

"That's what I came back for... The life I wanted. With you. The life you gave to someone else. To Sarah."

"Fuck," I fight back my own tears upon hearing her confession. There was a part of me that always knew. I ignored it, much like I ignored her, for the sake of my marriage.

Quinn's lower lip trembles for moment, and I know the question about to fall over her lips before she asks it. "Did you love her?"

"Yes." I tell the truth, knowing it might crush her.

"Like you loved me?"

"No. I loved...love...Sarah with my whole heart. I can't deny that." I hesitate before continuing, trying to unsuccessfully to collect my scattered, broken-hearted thoughts. "I don't know how to describe it, but I loved you both so deeply and so differently, yet both of you totally fucking ruined me."

"We've both ruined each other," Quinn sighs. "We're fucking toxic. Tumultuous. We both know that nothing good will come of the two of us being together."

Pushing back from the door frame, I stand in the middle of the hallway and stare at her for a moment before agreeing. *I can't argue with her rational thinking.* She's probably right. There is no denying that the two of us are absolutely chaotic together.

Just as much as there is no denying this bond between us. Decades and oceans couldn't tame what we feel for each other. It's not want or need It's like we're being pulled together, no matter how much we try to pull apart.

I make it three steps down the hall before she scoffs, "Besides, no one meets their soulmate when they're ten years old."

Her words cement my feet in place. I try to fight it, but as much as I will myself to walk, I can't bring myself to take another step from her.

"Fuck," I exhale. "But what if they do?"

I take a step backward and barrel through the open threshold, unable to close the distance between the two of us fast enough. My hands cup her face as I slide my fingers into her red locks before pulling her to my mouth. I pause for a second, but when I feel her pouty lower lip quiver against mine, I can't stop myself from sucking it between my teeth. Quinn lets out a faint whimper when I bite down on it, and I lose my resolve.

My lips crash into hers as I plunge my tongue between her lips. I plunder her mouth, exploring it and reclaiming it *as mine*, until both of us are breathless and panting with desire. She reaches between us and begins to unfasten my belt. I let her pull it from my pants before dropping us both to the mattress behind her. Gripping her wrists, I roughly yank them both above her head before pulling the belt from her hands. I cinch it around her wrists as she lets out a sweet moan that travels straight to my cock.

Breaking our kiss, I groan against her lips. "Is this how you want it?"

"Yes," she breathlessly answers.

CHAPTER NINETEEN
QUINN

Declan's lips pepper soft, wet kisses down the length of my neck. He reaches the crook and nips hard at the sensitive skin. "I don't think you do; is that how you address me?"

His touch has always excited me, but the way he has of demanding control sets my body on fire.

"No, Sir."

With his fingers and lips teasingly dusting over my skin, Declan rids me of my clothes, before taking off his own shirt. My eyes trail down his body, suddenly fixating more on the wounds marring his chest and stomach than I am on his physique. His scars document the rough life he's lived, the one he was so afraid of pulling me into.

"Do you remember our safe word?"

"Yes, Sir," I respond, and a look of pride spreads over his face as he climbs onto the bed and hovers over my body.

"I'd be lying if I didn't say I was worried that this will be too much for you," he shares, and there's concern growing in his eyes. The fleeting thought crosses my mind, but there's a difference between being held down against your will and voluntarily giving away full control of your body. There is a certain freedom that comes with submission, which is incomparable to anything else I have ever experienced. His fingers slip under my jaw, and his eye bore into my soul as he demands, "Promise me, you will not hesitate to use your safe word if you even remotely need me to stop."

His concern moves me to the point that I find myself choking back a sob as I whisper, "Always, Sir."

"Good girl." He places a soft kiss against my lips before climbing from me and walking to the foot of the bed.

Lifting my robe from the bench, he takes his time gathering the silk into his hands as he pulls the sash from the loops. He takes a hold of the belt between my wrists and gently pulls my hands to the footboard. Staring down at me, he slips the silk through the leather and secures the makeshift handcuffs to the iron bar with a simple hook knot.

The free end of the sash drags over my face and down my neck. He swirls the buttery fabric over my tight nipple, and I arch into the featherlight touch. It wisps over my stomach and flutters across the mound of my pussy. It's so delicate that I can barely feel it on my skin, yet I'm writhing and whimpering beneath it, feeling as though my body is ready to explode.

My skin burns with excitement as Declan slides his hand along the curve of my torso and under the back of my thigh. Hooking his fingers under my knee, he pulls it up to my hip and parts my thighs as the sash glides across my inner thigh. He slips the sash behind my knee and uses his grip on the fabric to keep me spread wide as he drags the knuckles of his free hand down my thigh.

"You're so fucking wet for me," he groans as his hand rubs over my pussy, and his fingers slide through the wetness dripping from me. He slides them over my lips, leaving a trail of arousal across them before plunging them into my mouth. He rubs them firmly over my tongue, covering it with my arousal. Now covered in saliva, he pulls them from my mouth and quickly replaces them with his tongue. He moans into my mouth as he licks the taste of my pussy from my tongue and eventually my lips. "I nearly forgot how fucking good you taste."

His saliva-covered fingers make their way to my clit and my dripping entrance. He rubs and thrusts them, causing my light whimpers to quickly turn into uncontrollable moans as he skillfully hurtles me toward the brink and holds me at the cusp.

"Please," I beg. "Please, Sir."

"Not yet." His fingers press in deep, and he slowly curls them as they firmly rub over the spot I know will do me in. Drawing my release ever closer, he kisses up my neck and presses his lips to my ear before whispering, "You're so fucking close that your tight little cunt is quivering around my fingers. You want to come so fucking badly, but you're going to be a good girl for me, aren't you? You're going to wait until I say you can."

I part my lips, wanting to answer him, but I'm unable to speak as every bit of my focus is being used to fight off my release. He stills his fingers for a second, and I manage to stammer, "Y...yes, Sir." He places a soft kiss to my forehead, silently praising me as he begins to work his fingers again. Slowly at first, but quickly working them toward a punishing pace. I cry out in pleasure as my orgasm fires through my nerves and shoots from me, spraying over the bed.

"Did I give you permission to come?" Declan smirks, tugging hard at the silk as his firm palm swats the release-covered mound of my pussy, causing me to gasp as the wetness splatters over my stomach and my bent leg is roughly hoisted closer to my shoulder.

"No, Sir," I answer, gasping for breath, both of us knowing full well that he wasn't stopping until he pulled an orgasm from me. Declan meticulously folds the silk fabric over itself until my leg is firmly secured to the silk sash being used to bind my hands to the foot of the bed.

"Now you've gone and made a mess of yourself and the bed," he taunts, climbing onto the bed with his fingers rubbing through the wetness on my stomach and thighs. When he settles between my splayed legs, his eyes roam over me and the damp sheets as he shakes his head, disappointed. He plunges his fingers into me and growls, "And do we remember what happens when we come before we're given permission?"

Fuck, I'm in trouble.

CHAPTER TWENTY
DECLAN

As I leisurely work my fingers in and out of her, I repeat my question, "What happens when you don't wait for her permission?"

"I get corrected, Sir." Quinn slides back into the role of my submissive with ease and comfort. *Like she never left.*

"Maybe I rub this little spot"—I smirk, leaning on her lower stomach and firmly curling my fingers upward along the soft, spongy part of her walls—"and make that pretty little pussy of yours gush until you've soaked us both."

Leaning forward, I lick through the sweet droplets of liquid on her stomach and down to her clit. "But... maybe denying you for hours will be a better reminder." She whimpers as I circle the tip of my tongue around her clit with a feathery touch at a torturously slow pace. Her hips buck, futilely seeking a heavier touch and my tongue *on* her clit.

"Or for being so eager"—my words vibrate against the swollen lips of her cunt—"I'll make you give me more of what you so greedily needed." *What I fucking need.* I dive face-first between her thighs, sucking her already sensitive clit into my mouth and massaging it with my tongue. Matching the slow rhythmic curl of my fingers, I place long, wet kisses against her cunt as I continue to sweep the flat of my tongue through her.

Her bound leg begins to tug at her binding as both of her thighs tremble uncontrollably. Breathy moans blow over her lips as she writhes against my mouth. She's on the brink and fighting so hard to stave off the orgasm I'm demanding from her. "Come for me." I kiss the demand against her between swipes of my tongue. "Come until you've soaked my face and the only thing you can think about is being filled with my cock."

Increasing the speed of my fingers, I demandingly suck on her hard little clit. She screams out in pleasure, her delicious release flooding my mouth and dribbling down my chin as she comes. The satisfaction I get from making her come causes me to groan against her, and she whimpers from the vibrations. I keep her coming on my fingers and tongue until her entire body is quivering, and she painfully whimpers, "I can't..."

"You can't?" I pull my glistening fingers from her and tenderly rub them over her sensitive pussy as I speak. "Does that mean you need to use your safe word? Or do you need a second to find your words so you can tell me what you want?"

The tight peaks of her nipples rise and fall with her fast, heavy breaths. With my eyes locked on hers, I wait patiently for her answer. "Your cock." The breathless words bubble from her lips. "I need your cock, Sir."

Unbuttoning my pants, I push them down my thighs and ask, "And where do you need it?"

"In my pussy," she exhales as I climb over her and press the thick head of my tip to her slick entrance.

"Tell me again," I demand, denying us both the pleasure of pressing inside of her.

"I need your cock in my pussy, Sir."

After resting my lips against hers, I inch my cock into her until I'm buried to the hilt. *Fuck! She feels better than I remember.* A smile tugs at my lips as I groan, "Such a naughty fucking mouth on such a good girl."

Claiming her mouth, I draw back my hips and slide back into her. I want to take my time. I want to go slowly and savor this moment, but I find my hips thrusting harder and faster as though they have a mind of their own. Relentlessly, I drive into her quivering cunt; grunts and moans fill the room as she comes again. She clenches around me, causing me to come, and a guttural moan billows from my lungs. "Fuuuuck!"

With my cock spasming, I ride out my release and pump into her until she's milked every drop of cum from me. "Fuck," I blurt in a brief moment of clarity. I wasn't prepared for this; there haven't been condoms in this house in years. I meant to pull out, but I couldn't have stopped if my life depended on it. "I shouldn't have come in you."

"It's okay," Quinn softly comforts me with a chuckle as I begin to undo the sash. "I'm not a nineteen-year-old virgin anymore, Declan. I'm a thirty-four-year-old woman; I have birth control handled."

"You shouldn't have told me that." I hesitate to undo the belt around her wrists as I wrap her legs around my waist. "Now I want to keep you tied up and fuck your tight little cunt until you're full of my cum."

Quinn's legs tighten around my waist, silently letting me know she wants more and pulling my already hardening cock against her.

She always was fucking insatiable.

Getting reacquainted with each other, we spend the rest of the day and the entire night in her bed. We fuck mercilessly—like we're making up for years in the span of a few hours. When I'm not buried inside of her, she's nuzzled against me with my arms wrapped around her, talking about everything and nothing until the moment our exhaustion overtakes us both.

"Walking away... The way I've fucking treated you since you moved in, trying to make you hate me because I knew I didn't have the strength to keep us apart." Quinn's face rests on my chest as I talk and leisurely dust my fingers over the curvature of her spine. "I was a fucking idiot, *mo chéadsearc.*"

Quinn lifts her head and props herself onto her forearms across my chest. Cocking her head to the side, she quips, "Maybe don't be a fucking idiot anymore, Sir."

For the first time in longer than I can remember, I let out a deep, hearty laugh as I cup her bratty little face. Pulling her down to me, I press my lips to hers so I can claim her mouth again.

CHAPTER TWENTY-ONE

QUINN

Straddling Declan's waist, with his arms wrapped tightly around me, he kisses my lips and grinds his hips against me. I whimper into his mouth as my stomach angrily growls with hunger.

"I guess we can't stay in this bed forever," Declan speaks through our kiss as he rolls me onto my back. "I'll go and start some breakfast."

After finding his boxer briefs on the floor, Declan disappears down the hall. Dishes clatter in the kitchen as I slide from bed and throw on his discarded T-shirt. I find him whisking a bowl of eggs beside the stove when I enter the kitchen, immediately catching his eyes.

"You look good in my clothes," he confesses, putting the bowl of beaten eggs on the counter. Gripping my waist, he hoists me onto the counter, and I gasp when the cool marble hits my bare ass and thighs. He lightly grips the shirt and gives it a little tug. "But you'd look better out of it."

"Dec, I need to eat."

"So do I," he growls, parting my knees and kissing up my thighs. I'm about to protest again when his tongue licks over my clit. As he fervently licks over my sensitive nub, he slides a hand under my shirt. He gives a slight twist of my nipple before palming my breast and gently pushing me onto my back. With the cold countertop on my back and my thighs resting on his shoulders, I grind against his tongue as he quickly brings me to the edge.

"Yes… Right there… You're going…to make me come," I pant, lacing my fingers into his hair and moving him to exactly where I need him. Electricity shoots through me. I come hard and breathlessly scream, "Oh fuck!"

"Oh, fuck!" Layla's startled voice echoes my cry, and I snap my eyes open to find her standing with her hands clamped over Fiona's eyes. I shove Declan from between my thighs and scrabble at the T-shirt to pull it back over my body.

"What's with all the screaming?" Jorge walks into the room with a bag of groceries as Declan wipes me from his face with the back of his hand. "Oh, fuck."

"We don't say that!" Fiona asserts from beneath the blindfold of Layla's hands.

I want to die now.

"I'm glad to see the two of you are feeling better," Layla chirps as she begins to usher Fiona out of the room.

Jorge snickers as he follows them. "Sometimes you just need a little Vitamin D."

Declan steps to the counter and cups my face before placing a soft kiss on my lips and helping me to my feet. "Go get dressed while I make your eggs. Maybe put on some panties this time," he instructs with a coy smile.

I don't hesitate to do as I'm told, eagerly looking forward to hiding in my room for a few minutes while I wait for my face to no longer be the same shade as a firetruck. After quickly cleaning up with a washcloth, I throw on a pair of leggings and a baggy shirt and head back into the living room to face the music.

Declan carries the plate of eggs to me, seemingly uncaring that he's semi-hard in his boxer briefs in front of Layla and Jorge. "Eat up." He hands me the plate and places a kiss on my forehead. "I've got to leave. Tristan called; he needs me over at the club."

"Girl, you better spill it," Jorge demands from the couch the second Declan disappears down the hall.

"Seriously!" Layla exclaims. "How didn't you tell me?"

"There wasn't anything to tell." I shovel eggs into my mouth to bide myself some time.

Declan returns from getting dressed and presses a kiss atop my head before whispering, "I wasn't done, and I do plan to pick up where we left off later tonight."

Layla and Jorge's eyes stay locked on me as Declan crosses the room to say goodbye to Fiona, only giving him attention as they watch him walk toward the door to leave.

"Nothing to tell?" Jorge scoffs, "That didn't look like nothing. And that gorgeous man had his whole face buried in your—"

Layla smacks his arm to silence him as her eyes dart to Fiona who is laying on the floor, coloring quietly. "So, this is new?"

"Yes," I answer between bites of food. "I mean, sort of."

Fuck, why did I say that?

"What do you mean, sort of?" Layla asks.

I proceed to spend the next couple of hours giving them both the play-by-play of my sordid history with Declan, the two of them hanging on every word as though they're enthralled in a soap opera. After answering a barrage of questions, Layla and Jorge stay a little longer to watch Fiona while I take a much-needed shower to clean up.

My thoughts wander through the past twenty-four hours. So much has happened—it feels surreal. Too good to be true, even.

Don't ruin this for yourself, Quinn.

CHAPTER TWENTY-TWO
DECLAN

When I walk into the club, I find all my brothers waiting in the lounge.

"What the fuck was so important I had to get down here right away?"

"This." Tris holds up a piece of paper with words scribbled across it in thick, black marker. Tristan hands it to me as I take a seat in the upholstered chair beside him.

YOU SHOULDN'T HAVE KILLED MY FATHER. UNLIKE HIM, I WON'T BE STOPPING AT THE RED-HEADED WHORE.

"Fuck!" I angrily crumple the paper into a tight ball and toss it across the room.

"Your reactions clears up a lot about the text I got as you pulled up."

"The text?" I ask.

"So, Layla wasn't fucking with him?" Liam blurts. "She really did walk in on you and Quinn."

I shake my head. "Fucking death threats left on the door, and the lot of you are still entirely focused on your unhealthy obsession with my sex life."

"You did!" Conor exclaims. "You fucked Quinn."

"It's about fucking time the two of you got back together," Finn announces, and jaws drop around the room as everyone falls silent. All eyes fixate on me before darting back to Finn. "You lot can't be fucking serious!"

Everyone continues to stare at Finn in disbelief, me included. "And *I'm* the one that never knows what's going on? Why do you think I always give you so much shit about her?" Finn asks rhetorically.

"How the fuck did you know?" I ask, inadvertantly admitting to his claims.

His eyes span across the gathering of chairs, looking at each of my brothers before asking, "How the fuck didn't everyone else? Have you fucking seen the way he looks at her? The way he's fucking looked at her since we were fucking teenagers. If you missed that, maybe you noticed how fucking miserable he was when she left for Ireland? Or when he took that trip to visit,"—he air quotes—"*Mam.* He went to see Quinn. Fuck, he was barely gone long enough to get through customs."

"You actually picked up on all that and figured out they were together?" Tristan huffs, confused.

"I mean... A few weeks before Quinn left for Ireland, I may have also caught them once when I broke into Dec's place in the middle of the night to,"—he air quotes again —"*borrow the keys to his car.*"

"You fucking twat." I shake my head. "And all this time, you didn't say a thing?"

 "Not my fucking place." Finn shrugs. His response gives me a newfound respect for him. Maybe he isn't the impulsively reckless twat I've always thought he was. His seriousness subsides, and he chuckles, "But I need to know. When you came, was it actually dust?"

Nope, respect gone, just like that.

Still a juvenile fucking twat.

My eyes fall to the crumpled paper on the floor. "They're going to come for her—"

"We'll put more men on her," Conor interjects.

"I won't let anything happen to her," I grit through my clenched teeth, angry at myself for putting her in this position once again with my recklessness. Killing Akim has only put a bigger target on her back. On the backs of everyone I love. "I'll do anything to keep her safe. And *a stóirín.* Everyone you all care about. And eventually, all of you."

"We will *all* do anything to keep her safe," Liam imparts as he gives my shoulder a reassuring squeeze.

Pulling my phone from my pocket, I shoot Rory a quick text.

> I need you at my apartment.

> *Inside* my apartment.

RORY

I can be there in five minutes.

Inside, sir?

> Yes. Use discretion. Fiona isn't to know anything is going on.

Of course.

> No one comes inside that isn't me or one of my brothers, understood?

Understood.

> I'll explain more when I get there.

Swiping through my contacts, I fire off another to Quinn.

> Are Layla and Jorge still there?

QUINN

Yeah.

> Tell them to stay with you. All of you stay inside. Do not leave the apartment, Quinn. Rory is on his way up to you.

You're scaring me.

> Good. That means you'll listen.

I'm leaving now.

"Layla is still at my place," I inform Tristan as I rise from my chair. "And Rory will be watching over them until we get there."

Tristan and I head to my Suburban, leaving Liam, Finn and Conor behind at the club. They will follow us to my place after sending the cleaning staff home and ensuring things are securely locked up. The last thing we need is the Bratva infiltrating our club, putting our livelihoods at risk—in addition to our family.

Reaching my apartment building, I am relieved to find everything appears to be normal. My relief doesn't waiver until I walk through the front door and am met with Quinn's anxious eyes. After crossing the room, I place a reassuring kiss on her forehead as Fiona excitedly shows me the picture she's drawing. "That's beautiful, *a stóirín!* I want you to tell me all about it after I talk with Rory, okay?"

"Okay, *daidi.*" She returns to her drawing, oblivious to the surrounding tension. Turning my attention back to Quinn, I whisper, "I need to talk to Rory, and then I'll explain everything. You, Fiona, Layla... All of you are perfectly safe here."

The anxiety in her eyes subsides slightly, but when I place a kiss against her trembling lips, it's clear that she is still afraid. The last thing she needed was more to worry about. She doesn't need more fuel to add to her nightmares. Tristan and I spend about an hour getting

Rory up to speed and devising a plan for increased security for the girls. By the time we finish, Conor, Liam and Finn have all arrived. The three of them graciously occupy Fiona while Tristan and I fill Quinn and Layla in.

"You promise they won't get to me?" Quinn asks, the nervous tremble still present in her voice.

"I promise, *mo chéadsearc*," I cup her face and stare down at her. "That is a promise I will *never* break to you again. I will die protecting you."

CHAPTER TWENTY-THREE
DECLAN

It's been nearly two weeks since the Bratva left their threat on the front door of the club, and not a thing has happened. Quite literally, not a thing—except the continued disruption to our more questionable business practices, mainly the unlicensed gambling, that have been nearly constant since this war started. There's been no more threats. No attacks on any of our men. At this point, I think we're all starting to think that it was nothing more than an idle threat.

Even me.

Of course, I've still kept Quinn and Fiona locked up in this apartment for their safety.

"She's finally back to bed. I didn't think I'd ever get her back to sleep!" I exclaim, wrapping my arms around Quinn from behind as she sits on the couch. I place a soft, wet kiss against the side of her neck, and my breath blows over her skin as I whisper, "What are the chances I can get *you* to come to bed?"

"Not too good," she brats, giggling as my tongue teasingly licks around the rim of her ear. I tighten my arms around her, and she squeals as I quickly climb over the couch and pin her to it face-down beneath me.

"Only not too good?" I huff, nipping along her neck. "I guess I'll just have to play with you here, then."

Firmly gripping her wrists with one hand and holding them above her head, I grasp the waist of her leggings. With one swift tug, I pull them and her panties down to her thighs. My hand rubs over the swell of her ass, and I growl, "If you want to come tonight, you're going to roll over and do exactly as I say. When I say."

She rolls onto her back, and I help to rid her of her pants, tossing them to the floor, and demanding, "Take off your top." After she pulls my shirt over her head, she tosses it to the floor beside the couch and lays down to await my next instructions.

"Good girl," I praise, sliding to the far end of the couch. "You look so fucking beautiful, *mo chéadsearc*. Place your hands on your tits and grab them."

She does as I instructed, kneading at her breasts. "Harder," I grunt. "Imagine they're my hands and how *I* would touch you."

She squeezes harder and her nipples become firm tight

peaks. I groan in delight as I unzip my pants. "That's better. Do my hands feel good on you?"

"Yes, Sir," she pants, pinching and tugging at both of her nipples.

"Show me. Use your hands to spread your thighs." She slides her hands down her stomach, approaching her always needy cunt, and I warn, "Don't you dare touch your pussy."

I languidly stroke my growing length as I watch her hands run along her inner thighs as she spreads herself wide for me. My gaze hungrily rakes over her body and down to her glistening cunt. "Wider. Show me how fucking wet you are." I pause to take in her sweet, pink perfection. "Such a good girl. A perfect little slut. I want you to show me what a good little slut you can be. Will you do that for me?"

"Yes, Sir." Her response is full of trepidatious excitement.

"Wrap your hand around your throat and place the other on your clit." She follows my commands without delay, and I croon, "What an obedient little slut you are. Listening so well and waiting for permission."

She lays still, her fingers resting on her clit, and her hand squeezing lightly around her throat. Sliding my fist along my cock, I instruct, "Don't move your hand. Roll your hips for me. Around and around. Grind your clit against your fingers. Now, stop!"

I firmly grip her wrist when she hesitates to obey my command, pulling it from her clit. "When I say 'stop,' you stop. Your pleasure is at my will. You don't come until you're told."

Releasing her hand, I place it back on her clit and give her permission to grind her hips again. "Can you feel yourself fucking dripping? Rub your fingers through it. Let me hear how fucking wet you are for me."

Her fingers rub over her pussy and audibly slide through her wetness. Watching her tease herself is fucking mesmerizing. "Rub *my* fucking pussy. Feel it fucking dripping as you rub your clit for me like the little slut you are. You look so fucking good, rubbing over clit for me. Keep rubbing your wet fucking pussy. Spread yourself and show me just how naughty you can be."

She spreads her pussy wider and teasingly rubs a finger around her entrance. "Are you needy for my cock? Tell me, and I'll let you fill that tight, needy cunt of yours."

"I need your cock," she eyes my fist, stroking over my length.

"Press your fingers into your cunt, nice and deep for me. You're going to fuck yourself. Hard. As fast as you can while I count from ten. Are you ready?" She nods her response. "Ten. Nine. That's it. Seven. Harder. Five. So fucking wet"—her fingers vigorously thrust into her slick cunt, and I groan as she works herself to the brink—"Three. Two. Stop."

She immediately stills her hand, panting with her eyes full of need.

"Good girl. Again. Ten. Nine. Eight. Seven. Imagine my thick cock stretching out that tight little hole"—Quinn groans as her hand plunges between her thighs—"Five. Four. You need my cock. Three. Fuck your pussy as I watch. Two. Stop."

My hips thrust into my hand, needing to be inside of her as much as she wants me there.

CHAPTER TWENTY-FOUR

QUINN

This is fucking blissful torture.

"Do you feel how fucking wet you are for me? How fucking badly you want me?" he taunts. "Five seconds. I want you right at the edge."

I thrust my fingers into my pussy as he counts, "Five. Four. Fuck yourself for me like the little slut you are. Two. Keep going. Don't stop. Right to the edge. That's it. Stop."

My pussy clenches around my fingers, demanding more as Declan groans from his own strokes. Both of us are fighting against an unbearable need to come as he continues to direct my edging. "Again. Five more seconds. Five. Four. Watch me stroke my cock for you. Two. Harder. Yes. Stop."

"Please, Sir," I beg as I watch Declan strip from his clothes. "Please let me come."

"Such a good girl. Begging for what you need." He beams down at me with pride. "One more time. Let me watch you rub your clit, and when I get to one, you can come."

Pulling my slick fingers from inside me, I place them on my clit and impatiently wait for Declan to start counting again. He settles himself between my thighs and whispers, "Ten."

Fucking ten?

"Nine. Good girl. Show me how you like it. Seven. Yes. Harder. Six."

My back arches from the couch, and guttural moans pass over my trembling lower lip as I struggle not to come.

"Fuck, yes. You're going to come so fucking hard for me. Every bit of you exploding. Five. Knowing that I'm going to fuck that needy cunt with my cock. Four. Don't you dare fucking come. Three. Rub your clit. Keep going. Two. Now, fucking come for me, Quinn."

The release building at my core spasms violently through my body, screams rattling from my lungs as Declan slams himself into me. He thrusts at a punishing pace, grunting, "Don't you dare fucking stop. Keep rubbing your clit as you take my fucking cock and come all over me."

"Dec!" I scream as another orgasm rushes through me.

"Fuck... My fucking pussy feels so fucking good," he groans the words as a never-ending string of orgasms shoots through me. "So fucking good, quivering around my cock. Be my good girl and keep coming all over me."

Declan grows even more rigid, the head of his cock dragging along the most sensitive parts of me until there's nothing left of me but a quivering, breathless puddle beneath him.

"Oh...fuck...." he grunts as his sweat-covered body crumples onto mine, both of us completely exhausted.

We lay in silence, our labored breaths and the ticking of the clock on the mantel the only sounds in the room. My eyelids grow heavy as Declan holds me in his arms, his lips dusting against my forehead.

"You aren't just a good girl," Declan wakes me, peppering kisses over my cheeks as he strokes the sweaty hair from my face. "You are *my* perfect, good fucking girl. So fucking perfect for me."

My heart swells, and a lump grows in my throat from the way he stares down at me. It's soon—*so fucking soon*—but I'm barely awake and can't stop the words from blowing over my lips. "I love you." Declan continues to gaze into my eyes in total silence, and that lump in my throat morphs into panic. "I am sorry. I know it's too soon. I shouldn't have said—"

"Shhh. You know who you are to me. Who you've always been... *Mo cheadsearc.*" Declan kisses my lips before continuing, "My first love. I love you. I've *always* loved you."

He presses his lips to mine and slips his tongue between them. His tongue sweeps around my mouth with slow, languid strokes. There is no haste or need. It's soft and gentle—filled with his adoration—as his hands slide over my body and he pulls himself tighter to me.

Declan rolls on top of me and presses his hard length into me. When I wince from the slight discomfort from earlier, he stills, asking, "Are you sore?"

"Yes," I whisper, trying to relax.

"I'll go slowly." He rocks his hips, inching himself in and out of me, holding true to his word. "I want to take my time and enjoy every leisurely stroke knowing that you're mine."

"I'm yours," I whisper against his chest as he continues to slide into me. His lips and hands roam over my skin, setting me afire in ways he never has before. "I've always been yours, Declan. I always will be."

Our arms and legs are so tightly wrapped around one another, I no longer know where he stops and I begin. We are completely lost in each other by the time he brings us both over the edge.

Declan lifting me into his arms jostles me awake with a startle. "You're okay. I've got you," he kisses my forehead as he pulls my naked body against his. "I'm just taking us to bed."

I cling to him as he carries me through the apartment in

the dark. He pours us both into bed and pulls the blankets over us as I nuzzle into him.

He pulls me in even tighter, until there isn't room for air between us. With his arms wrapped firmly around me, I quickly drift back to sleep.

"I love you, *mo cheadsearc.*"

CHAPTER TWENTY-FIVE
DECLAN

Sarah's eyelids flutter, and she tries to lift her heavy head from the pillow. She's been asleep for most of the afternoon, the time she spent holding Fiona this morning having absolutely exhausted her. Her voice cracks, whispering my name, as she searches the room for me. "Declan?"

"I'm right here." I quickly cross the room and gently squeeze her hand as soon as I reach her bedside. No matter how hard it is being here, wild horses couldn't pull me away from her.

Without letting go of her hand, I pull up my chair and sit beside her. Her grip on my hand has grown drastically weaker this past month, matching the current frailty of her body. She's so thin, I can't imagine she still even weighs one hundred pounds. The drugs, previously prolonging her life, have now done nothing but cause absolute havoc on her body.

A navy-blue silk scarf is wrapped around her head, providing warmth and a semblance of self from the when the chemotherapy caused her to lose most of her gorgeous strawberry-blonde hair. Those same chemicals coursing through her veins have left her previously perfect porcelain skin riddled with bruises and scarred from chemo's painful scarlet rash. Even now, a shell of who she was a year ago, Sarah is still fucking beautiful.

"Promise me," she forces the words through her shallow breaths, "Promise me you'll be the father I know you can be." Squeezing her hand, I promise even though I have no idea how to raise a child on my own nor have the faith in myself that she had in me to do it.

Neither of us is under any notion that a miracle is coming. Treatments have failed her, and we moved her from the hospital a few days ago so that she could die at home in peace. As I watch the numbers dwindle on monitors beside her bed, I know we are at the end. I know I am about to lose her.

Struggling to turn on her pillow to face me, she asks the same question I've heard every day since we learned that her cancer was terminal. "Will you love me for the rest of my life?"

The numbers continue to fall on the monitor as I stand. I gently lift the oxygen mask from her face and place a kiss on her lips as the alarms sound to alert the at-home nurse that her heart has stopped. The tears in my eyes fall upon her cheeks as I press my forehead to hers, answering her question seconds too late. "No, mo grah, I'll love you for the rest of mine."

Startling awake, I wipe the tears from my face. Every bit

of my dream was so vivid; it was like living through it all over again.

Losing her all over again.

The bed shifts as Quinn burrows herself against me, and I am slammed with guilt like I have never felt before. I promised Sarah I'd love her forever, and I'm lying in our bed with another woman. Pulling my arm from under her, I push back the navy duvet and climb from the mattress.

"What's wrong?" Quinn's groggy voice cracks. Pacing along the floor-to-ceiling windows and staring over the city skyline, I hesitate to answer her question. When I don't, she climbs out of bed to join me at the window. She reaches out to wrap her arms around me and I grab her wrists to stop her.

I don't deserve it.

I have been lucky—or unlucky—enough to love two women in my life. Not only have I had to deal with the pain of losing both of them, but I'm now riddled with guilt over not maintaining my promises to either of them.

"Declan," Quinn delicately demands my attention. "Look at me."

The faint lights of the skyline illuminate her face and the gold flecks in her emerald eyes twinkle in the dim light of the room. She stares up at me, her gaze unwavering as she sniffles, "Don't shut me out. Don't push me away. If you do, you will break me. Mourning us again will break me in ways I will never recover from."

"Quinn..." I sob as I wipe the tear rolling down her cheek.

"I love you." She palms my face with both hands. "Let me in. Let me help you with whatever you are struggling with."

"I'm sorry," I apologize into the void. "I promised to take care of you. I promised to love her. I've done nothing but fail you both."

"You did not fail me, Declan. Shitty things happen in this world, and as much as you will it, you cannot always protect everyone you love." She squeezes my face harder and looks deep into my soul. "And you *did not* fail Sarah."

"But—"

"No. Listen to me," Quinn interrupts. "Life ends. Love doesn't. I know you love her, and I know you always will."

Quinn slides her hands from my face to my chest and rests them over the thud of my heart. "I don't need you to love her less to make room in here for me, just like you didn't forget about me to make room for her. I know that your heart is plenty big enough to have room for us both because it always has."

She slides her arms around me and holds me tight. With her face resting against my chest, I mutter, "I will never grasp how you can be so understanding of...everything."

"It's simple. The stupid decisions you've made, your pain, your faults, Sarah, Fiona... All of them have made the version of you finally ready to let me in... To love me."

"I do," I whisper against her forehead. "I fucking love you, *mo cheadsearc.*"

"I love you, baby."

CHAPTER TWENTY-SIX
QUINN

About a month later...

"Alrighty, kiddo." I give Fiona a big push on the swings. "I think it's time to head inside so I can make you something for dinner."

"Two more!" she shouts.

"One more, but that's it...." I give her a final push, and she squeals as the swing goes high. She kicks her feet, trying to keep the swing going as it begins to slow. It might not be helping, but it sure is adorable. I wait until it comes to a stop before helping her down.

Taking her hand and walking inside, I ask, "What do you think we should make for dinner tonight?"

"Can we have pizza?" Fiona chirps as I close the door to the terrace.

"Hmmm. Let me text your dad and see if he's coming home soon." I reach for my back pocket, only to realize I left my phone by the slide of her swing set after taking a few pictures of her to send to Declan.

Leaving Fiona to play in the living room, I head back onto the terrace to retrieve it and call Declan.

"Hey, baby," I greet him when he answers the phone. "A cute little redhead is asking to have pizza for dinner."

His laugh billows through the speaker as he teases, "Is it the cute little three-foot-tall one? Or the cute little five-foot-tall one?"

"Both. If it means I don't have to cook dinner, it is definitely both."

"You know I'm not capable of saying no to either of you," he admits. When I step back inside, I immediately notice that Fiona isn't where I left her in the living room. Declan's voice continues to carry through the phone's speaker, but I'm distracted by the ding of the elevator in the foyer.

It's never that loud.

Except when we're in the foyer.

Quickly, I rush around the corner and gasp when I see that the front door of the apartment is open. I drop the phone, running toward the open doorway as I scream, "Fiona!"

With my heart pounding, I lunge through the threshold and into the foyer. Relief momentarily washes over me when I see her, but it quickly dissipates when I realize she's waving to someone as the metal doors slide closed.

Rushing toward her, I drop to the floor and firmly grip her arms, roughly admonishing, "What are you doing?"

Tears immediately well in her eyes, and I realize that I've scared her as much as she did me. I only scare her further when I hear the whir of the elevator motor and see the display over the cab is only at the floor beneath us.

The bell announcing the cab's arrival dings as I swoop Fiona into my arms. I hastily carry her back to the apartment and slam the door as a thick Russian accent taunts, "You can't hide from us forever, you redheaded bitch."

It isn't until I lock the deadbolt that I realize tears are streaming down both of our faces, and I'm trembling as hard as Fiona.

I run through the apartment and fall to the floor by my phone. Somehow, I clamor to lift it from the hardwood, and I yell for Declan and plead him to hurry home. Clutching the phone tightly, I find the line dead when I lift it to my ear.

My tears mirror Fiona's as I pull her into my lap. I hold her close to me, trying to comfort us both as my heart continues to pound in my chest. *That voice. It sounded just like them.* Unable to shake the visions of bar racing through my thoughts, I rock back and forth, repeating, "I'm so sorry, kiddo. I didn't mean to scare you."

A loud thud hits and vibrates the front door. I scream and clutch Fiona to my chest as it thuds again, the force so strong that it causes a picture of the boys to fall from the wall and crash against the floor. A third hit causes the wood frame to splinter, and the door violently swings inward on its hinges. Declan barrels through the open threshold, his gun drawn, with four men immediately on his heel. Terror laces his voice as he yells, "Quinn! Fiona!"

"Dec," I sob from where I sit on the floor, shielding Fiona's eyes.

Declan runs through the apartment and continues to shout our names. Finding us on the floor, he shoves his gun into the back of his pants and drops to his knees beside us. His arms wrap around us both, pulling us painfully tight as he plants kisses across our faces. "Thank fucking God."

"*Daidi*," Fiona cries, pulling from my hold and crawling into his arms.

"It's okay, *a stóirín*." He pulls her into his embrace. "You're okay."

Holding her firmly against him with one arm, he keeps the other wrapped around me. "You're both okay," his fear-filled eyes meet mine. "Both my girls are okay."

Sucking in a shaky breath, I hold his gaze and silently shake my head. *I am currently very much not okay.* The fear I had for myself didn't hold a flame to how terrified I was that something would happen to Fiona.

"The building is clear, sir," Rory announces when he barges into the room.

"I need you to stay with Quinn for a moment, *a stóirín*." Declan gives Fiona a squeeze and passes her back into my lap. He places a tender kiss on my forehead before pushing himself from the floor and to his feet.

He calmly crosses the room, pausing a few feet from Rory to glance back at me. While his demeanor is calm, I've seen that look in his eyes before. It's the same way he reacted years ago at the frat party.

Rage. Uncontrollable rage.

I turn Fiona's face away from him, and I cover her ear with my palm as I press the other to my chest.

Declan glares at Rory as he closes the last couple of feet between them, fisting his shirt and driving him violently into the wall when he reaches him. Spittle sprays from Declan's mouth and over Rory's face, as he snarls, "How the fuck this happen? How in the *fuck* did they almost get to my family?"

CHAPTER TWENTY-SEVEN
DECLAN

Shoving my forearm into Rory's throat, I pin him to the wall with the weight of my body. Struggling to breathe, he chokes out, "They came up the back. They took out Nolan and Sully."

"My family!" I seethe, my body coursing with equal parts fear and rage. Balling my fist, I throw a punch into his gut, forcing him to blow out a heavy groan. His body attempts to bend to ease the pain, only causing him to choke harder on my wedged arm still against his windpipe. "They almost got to my fucking family!"

My home is a fucking fortress. Men surround this building day and night, watching over everything. *Everyone.* There isn't an inch of this place not monitored by security cameras. Making it this far, to my floor—to *my* front fucking door—is not something that any of my enemies should ever be able to do.

"Where the fuck were you?" I snark, pulling the gun from my waistband. I shove the muzzle under Rory's jaw with enough anger that he winces as his head snaps upward. He's the best man I have. He's been with me for years, and in charge of ensuring the safety of my family since before Fiona was born. I trust him to keep them all safe when I can't.

Trusted him.

Rory opens his mouth to explain, but he's pinned so firmly beneath my forearm that he can barely breathe, let alone speak. Yet, his lack of response only fuels my ire. Grinding the muzzle into the skin under his jaw, I snarl, "Where the fuck were you? You're supposed to fucking protect them!"

Failing me and my family isn't just disappointment. It's fucking betrayal. You don't betray the Evans brothers because there is only one punishment. *Death.*

Flipping off the safety on my pistol, my index finger flexes against the trigger. Rory doesn't try to yell. There are no sobs or tears of a man about to meet his maker unwillingly. Instead, he stands tall and holds my gaze, ready to receive what he knows is coming.

"Declan!" Quinn shouts from behind me. With my arm still wedged tightly against Rory and the trigger half-cocked, I turn my head. I find her standing several feet from me with Fiona protectively wrapped around her. She stares at me silently for a moment before softly pleading, "Stop."

Her emerald eyes are unwavering, and I cannot pull away from her gaze. Staring at her, I find my heated breaths slowing to match hers as my misplaced rage begins to subside.

"Let him go," Quinn gently insists. "You know he's not responsible. He would do anything to keep us safe, and you know it."

My hands fall to my sides, pulling the gun from Rory's jaw and my arm from his throat. He crumples to the floor, choking and desperately sucking in the air that I had been denying him. Drawing in a deep breath, he looks up from his crouched position on the floor. His eyes full of gratitude. "Thank you," he heaves, looking at Quinn.

Stowing my gun in my waistband, I watch as Rory climbs from the floor. He swallows hard and rubs at his throat. His voice is hoarse, but he answers my questions. "I was in the lobby, sir. You had an unexpected delivery that needed to be dealt with."

"A delivery?" I inquire, knowing that I am not expecting any packages.

Rory lifts his hand, offering me a piece of paper that I didn't previously realize he was holding. Passing it to me, he shares, "It was attached to the box."

"Box of what?" I huff.

Rory lowers his voice. "Photographs."

Unfolding it, I immediately recognize it is the same handwriting as the note we had deemed an idle threat at the club.

NOW YOU KNOW HOW EASILY I CAN GET TO THOSE YOU CARE ABOUT. NEXT TIME I WON'T BE LEAVING WITHOUT THE WHORE.

"Photos of what?" Quinn hesitantly asks, clearly unsure if she wants to know the answer to her own question.

Rory pulls his phone from his pocket and sends a text. A few minutes later, the elevator dings, and one of his guys arrives with a decorative black box and a red silk ribbon. He hands both to Rory, who then places them on the counter before me.

Lifting the lid, I toss it onto the white marble counter. I take a quick glance inside, and my eyes dart to Quinn before turning to Rory. "How the *fuck* did they get these?" I bark.

"I gave the order to shut it down the moment I saw it," Rory informs me. "They should be looking now to see how anyone managed to get access in the first place."

"When they find it, I want whoever is responsible," I snarl.

"Of course, sir," Rory nods.

Quinn steps closer and passes me Fiona before reaching for the box.

"Don't." I shake my head, but it's too late.

She lifts a handful of the photographs from the box with a gasp, tossing each to the counter after she looks at them. Hundreds of pictures of her—*of us*—in compromising positions. All of them, from the confines of this apartment and pulled from the security cameras covering every inch of this place.

"Dec?" she gulps.

I reach forward and place my hand on her back, trying to comfort her. We agreed shortly after she moved in that the cameras would stay. Access to footage is very limited, but even the men monitoring the cameras don't have access to moments spread across the counter. If I don't turn off their access to the room we are intimate in, they have been instructed to do it themselves. *No one gets to see her like that without her consent.* Rubbing my hand along her back, I mutter, "I'm sorry."

"Not me." Her voice cracks as she lifts the photo in her hand for me to see.

"How in the fuck did no one catch this?" I snatch the photo from Quinn and shove it at Rory.

CHAPTER TWENTY-EIGHT
QUINN

"I don't, Sir. But I'm damn sure going to find out," Rory promises, staring at the photo and shaking his head in disbelief. Without another word to either of us, he storms from the apartment as he yells into his phone.

Somehow, I continue to rifle through the box, and there are more. *So many more.* Picture after picture of Fiona sleeping in her bed with a masked man standing over her. Some he's just watching. In others, he's holding a knife in his hands or pointing a gun at her head.

"He's been here...," I stammer, taking in the details of the photos, "a lot." His clothes don't change. In every photo, the man is wearing a black-on-black suit with a white ski mask covering his face, but Fiona is in at least six different sets of pajamas. He's been here—while we were sleeping down the hall—no less than six times.

"We came as fast as we could." Declan's brothers startle me when they all come barreling through the broken front door. *At this point, a random creek of the hardwood floor would probably cause me to panic.*

"How's my little nugget?" Conor croons, lifting Fiona from Declan's hold and positioning her on his hip. "I've been hearing so much about this fancy swing set you got, and not once have you invited me over to play."

"*Uncail* Conor, you're too big." Fiona shakes her head and a tiny smile tugs at the corner of her mouth. A tiny smile that I think all of us are relieved to see.

"Nonsense!" Conor huffs, even though his broad frame is truly way too big to fit through her play set. "I'll prove it."

"You're gon' get stuck," she flatly informs him as he lowers her to the ground, allowing her to take his hand and drag him onto the terrace.

These Evans men, all of them, absolutely amaze me. Their whole lives, they have destroyed anything that got in their way and done deplorable things to protect each other and their businesses. Yet, all five of them have an unwavering softness when it comes to those they love, and they would do *anything* to ensure the happiness of that little girl. I'm surprised women aren't falling on their backs and throwing their legs in the air to have these men father their children.

Scratch that—they all constantly have women on their backs. Among other positions.

"He is going to get stuck," I echo as Liam pulls me into him.

"And how's my little nugget?" he teases, and I shove him from me.

"I am *not* your little nugget," I huff with a chuckle.

"Based on these," Finn continues, rifling through the photos spread across the counter, "she ain't so little."

His statement draws everyone else's attention to the pornographic spread. And I'm less than thrilled to know that three of Dec's brothers now know exactly what I look like naked, bent over the couch, coming, riding their brother, *and* hog-tied.

"*Gnéasach*. Nice," Finn drags out the words as he lifts a photo of Delcan fucking my face while I'm suspended in an Agura tie. "And great use of that swing set."

Declan punches him—*hard*—in the arm and snatches the photo out of his hand before gathering the rest of them and shoving them back into the box.

"What?" Finn huffs, rubbing his arm. "You're the one fucking her on the terrace for the whole city to see, and *I* get a punch for looking at the picture a little too long?"

"There are pictures of Declan fucking Quinn?" Conor outstretches both palms, impatiently waiting for someone to pass one to him.

"You already fucked Tristan's wife. You don't need to see mine, too," Declan huffs, and my eyes snap toward him.

He doesn't even know what he just said.

Declan splays the letter on the counter, and everyone reads it, Finn with his lips moving.

"The three of you can't stay here," Tristan chimes. "It isn't safe."

"None of our places are going to be safe, though." The truth behind Declan's words is a little terrifying. "There are hundreds of people in and out of all our buildings every day. It's too easy for people to slip in unnoticed."

"You can't be thinking about staying here," Liam exclaims as he gestures toward the front door that's now hanging by a single hinge.

"He's been in this house. He's been watching us for months. I can't imagine he hasn't used that to his advantage. That he doesn't have a plan to get what he wants."

Me.

Declan pulls his phone from his pocket and makes a call as he paces toward the terrace to check on Fiona. Tristan, Liam, Conor, and Finn quibble about the situation, but my focus is entirely on Declan and listening to one side of his call. "Is it ready?—It needs to be ready by tonight —I want men there within the hour—I'm not asking, Rory—We'll be leaving here within the hour—And make sure the swing set is moved by morning."

I walk toward the windows lining the terrace, and Declan pulls me into him. He squeezes me—almost unbearably—tight and places a kiss against my forehead. "I'm not leaving your side, *mo chéadsearc.* You and *a stóirín*... I'll protect you both. No one will ever get that close to either of you again. I promise."

CHAPTER TWENTY-NINE
DECLAN

After zipping my packed suitcase, I pull it from the bed. Quinn helped with packing Fiona's things first, her rainbow suitcase at the door waiting to be loaded into the car. Quinn is currently filling a bag with a few days' worth of her necessities; enough clothes and toiletries to go away for a long weekend. Someone can come back to get more later.

If we come back.

"I'm going to put this one by the door"—I lift my suitcase—"and then grab a few things from my office."

"Okay." She nods, continuing to rummage through the drawers in the bathroom. "I should be ready to go in a few minutes."

Tristan left a bit ago, heading back to his place. He went under the guise of getting Layla and packing their things as well, but I know damn well that he's as concerned for her safety as I am for Quinn's and Fiona's. Conor, Liam, and Finn stayed behind to keep Fiona occupied while we quickly prepared to leave. They'll go to each other's places, respectively pack their things, and then join us later tonight.

Entering my office, I close the frosted French door behind me. The loose floorboard creaks as I walk along the wall of bookshelves before taking a seat in the high-backed leather chair behind the walnut desk. Running my hand along the bullnose of the desk, I unlock and open the drawer. It contains nothing but a small gift box. I pull it out and sigh.

This wasn't how this was supposed to go.

Pulling the bow undone, I drop the thin strand of white silk on the desk and open the little red leather box. I let it fall to the desk as I take out what was supposed to be Quinn's gift in just a few short days. Turning the key over in my hand, I stare at the silver keychain attached to it. I rub my thumb over the engraved inscription. *Build a life with me and fill this home with more love than it could possibly hold.*

I bought it for her—*for us*—a couple of weeks ago and have been keeping it a secret while crews work tirelessly to complete some remodeling and a few necessary security updates. With six bedrooms, the gated estate on the New Rochelle waterfront is going to be a big home for us to fill. *A task I am very much looking forward to.* Big inside and out, it has a private beach and a large yard for kids to play without armed guards hovering over them.

Everything about it was going to be perfect.

It was supposed to be a start to our new life—*the one she deserves*—not a sanctuary for my entire fucking family.

A soft rap at the door pulls me from my thoughts. I hastily grab the box and ribbon, dropping both into the drawer as the door to the office swings open. I shove the key into my pocket as Quinn steps through the threshold. "I think we're all set."

I'm about to stand from my chair when she closes the door behind her. Worried, I ask, "Are you okay?"

"I can't shake the worry." Her response is soft as she shakes her head. Crossing the room, she pushes my chair back from the desk. She gathers the floral fabric of her long dress into her fists, and I watch it lift inch-by-inch to her mid-thigh. Without saying a word, she climbs onto my lap, straddling me. I slide my hands along the smooth skin of her legs, stopping where the hemline rests high on her thigh. Placing her hands over mine, she drags them under her dress until I'm cupping her bare ass. "What are you doing, *mo chéadsearc?*"

"I need to feel something good." She moves her hips, and the warmth of her pussy radiates to my cotton-covered erection as she slowly grinds against me. Her hands work between us, needily pulling at my belt. She undoes my pants and slides her hand into them. A moan vibrates in my throat as her palm slides along my length, causing my cock to grow hard. "I want to feel...in control."

"Quinn…" I grip her wrist to stop her from stroking me, surprising even myself. Cupping her face, I'm about to tell her that this isn't a good idea. Everyone is waiting for us, and we need to leave this cursed apartment. But when I meet her gaze, I can't. Her emerald eyes are full of a mixture of pain and need, and I would do anything to ease even a little of either.

Even if it means relinquishing control.

"Ride my cock," I gravelly whisper, pulling her face toward mine. "Use me. Take what you want. Later, I'll give you what it is you actually need."

Gripping the base of my rigid shaft, Quinn groans as she presses my tip into her cunt. Her hips swirl, stretching her around me and quickly burying me to the hilt. She rides me hard, desperately seeking relief. The whimpers trembling over her lips grow into moans as the movements of her hips become more frantic.

"You look so fucking beautiful hovering on the edge as you ride my cock." I dust my finger over her plump lower lip, and she wraps her mouth around it. Sucking it hard, her lips slide from fingertip to knuckle as she continues to bounce over my cock. Her already tight cunt squeezes around me, and I can't stifle my groan. Quinn comes hard, swallowing my finger to silence her screams. Pulling my digit from her mouth, I press my lips to hers. "You're even more beautiful when you come undone."

Gripping her hips, I lift her to slide her from my still-rigid cock. Leaving it covered with her arousal, I tuck it back into my pants as her brows furrow. "Sir?"

"If you feel better, we're done—for now." I kiss the words against her lips. Pulling back, I meet her gaze and stare into her eyes. "I'll come later. Only after I take care of you and give you what you need."

CHAPTER THIRTY

QUINN

Declan spends nearly all the drive on the phone with Rory and Tristan, the three of them practically speaking in code, so I don't understand. With nothing else to do, I stare out the window, reading the signs and watching the city grow smaller with each passing mile.

By the time Declan is finally off the phone, we pull up to a tall, wrought-iron gate. He rolls down the window and pushes the buttons on the call box, causing the gate to open. We pass through and drive toward the massive home.

It's gorgeous!

Absolute overkill for an Airbnb to be used as a safehouse, but still gorgeous.

The sprawling mansion before me is modern and minimalist. Instead of being boxy with shutters and flower boxes, like most of the homes we passed as we drove through the suburbs, this one has curves and walls of windows overlooking the beautifully maintained yard. With its sculpturesque shape and the oversized black front door, it looks like a home out of a magazine.

"She's out cold, Dec," I murmur after glancing into the backseat when he pulls to a stop in the driveway. Normally, I would want to wake her, but she already ate dinner. The boys made sure their favorite little niece got the pizza she wanted while we were all still at the apartment. I'm a little worried that I'll never get her back to sleep because she's had a day.

We all have.

"It's okay. I'll get her," Declan whispers before climbing from the car. He carefully helps her out of her car seat in the backseat and pulls her into his arms without waking her. With Fiona's head resting on his shoulder, he leads me toward the front door. "Shit," he huffs. "The key for the house is in my pocket."

Reaching into his pocket, I playfully search for a little longer than needed before retrieving the key. Unlocking the door, I push it open and shove the key into the pocket of my sweatshirt. Declan walks through the dimly lit house with a clear destination in mind. I follow behind him, very surprised when we arrive at a pale-purple bedroom filled with all of Fiona's favorite things.

Probably all three-year-old girls' favorite things.

With Fiona still in Declan's arms, the two of us work together to clear the bed of stuffed animals, pull back the rainbow-printed covers, and tuck her in. We both place a few extra kisses on her forehead before leaving.

"I'm going to grab our bags," Declan quietly informs me as he shuts the door to the bedroom. When he reaches the stairs, he whisper-shouts, "Our room is the one with the double doors at the end of the hall."

Walking toward what is going to be our room for the duration of our stay, I glance through the open doors. All of the rooms have floor-to-ceiling windows overlooking to beach, illuminating them with moonlight. Each of them is empty, excluding some remnants of painting supplies.

Pushing open the double doors, I step into a stunning master bedroom and feel along the wall until I find a light switch. A tiny gasp blows over my lips when I flip it on.

Like the other rooms, an entire wall is built from windows overlooking the water. The other walls are deep charcoal, with matching trim work and minimalist sconces spread along them. All the furniture is black, decorated with dark-gray linens and throw pillows. It's dark, but the light bamboo floors and plants somehow make it feel welcoming.

Pulling off my sweatshirt as I stare over the water, something clatters against the hardwood floor. Looking down, I realize that I've dropped the front door key. I read the engraving on the keychain as I pick it up.

Build a life with me and fill this home with more love than it could possibly hold.

Declan startles me when he drops his car key on the dresser. Turning around, I timidly ask, "Dec? Whose house is this?"

"You weren't supposed to find out like this," he dodges my question as he closes the distance between us. Slipping his fingers under my chin and tipping my face up toward his, he stares at me in silence. The moonlight dances across his eyes like it's flickering over the ocean, and they have a sparkle to them as he says, "It's yours, *mo chéadsearc.*"

"This house is gorgeous, but it's way too big, Dec. We don't need this much space."

"I'm not just giving you a home. I'm asking you to grow a big, beautiful family with me, filling this house with little versions of you. I want everything with you, *mo chéadsearc.* With you as my wife."

"Yes," I muster the response as tears trickle down my cheeks. Declan kisses them away as he pulls me into his embrace. His peppered kisses fall over my lips, the soft, wispy kisses growing languid. Declan kisses me slowly and deeply, and I moan into his mouth as he presses me against the cool glass wall.

His fingers deftly ball my dress into his fists until it's around my waist and my bare ass is pressed against the cold sheet of glass. His lips trail up and down my neck, leaving a trail of wet kisses and the sting of tiny nips from his teeth. Reaching between us, Declan rubs the palm of his hand over my pussy.

"First, I'm going to take care of you and give you what you need, like I promised." He slides his fingers inside of me and works them at a leisurely pace as he continues to kiss up my neck. Reaching my ear, he presses his lips to it and whispers, "When I know you're good, I'm going to spend the night filling you with cum as I fuck my babies into you."

CHAPTER THIRTY-ONE
DECLAN

Quinn's arousal drips down my fingers as I fuck her with them. I work them slow and teasingly, taking my time building her right to the edge before stilling my hand.

"Show me how badly you want it. Grind over my hand like you rode my cock." I kiss the words along her neck and over her breasts.

With her shoulders pressed firmly against the glass, she rocks her hips. She slides repeatedly over my fingers, and the sounds of her wetness fill the room when she increases her tempo. With my hand around her throat, I lean back to watch her make my fingers disappear into her. I tighten my grip and groan, "So fucking needy. Let me watch you come for me."

Given permission, the gyrations of her hips become spasms, and euphoria washes over her face. Pulling my fingers from her, I shove them through her parted lips and rub them firmly over her tongue. Urging her to suck herself from me, I use my hold on her throat to lead her across the room.

"On your knees," I demand and gently push her toward the floor beneath the large eye-hook secured to the ceiling. She obediently falls to her knees and bows before me. I tenderly rub my saliva-coated fingers along her jaw. She stares up at me with wanting eyes, eager to please me. A look that makes me feral and leaves me struggling to maintain the control that I know she needs from me.

"I need you"—I bend down and place a wet, sloppy kiss on her lips— "bound and at my mercy. Letting me use you so I can show you just how in control of yourself you are."

Quinn doesn't move as I walk to the upholstered bench at the foot of the bed. Lifting the lid, I sift through the contents to retrieve three thirty-foot sections of hemp rope, a wand, and a hair tie. I place the rope and wand on the floor beside Quinn, then use the elastic band to secure her hair so it's out of the way while I bind her. I pace around her, undoing the buttons of my shirt as I admire how beautiful she is as she waits for me. Letting it fall to the floor, I kneel behind her.

"I want you to focus on my touch, on how I feel. I want you to enjoy every second." Pulling her back to my bare chest, I dust my fingers over her skin. They drag repeatedly from her neck to her thighs as she melts into my touch. Sliding my hand between her slightly parted thighs, I rub over the mound of her pussy. "I want you to come as you please, showing me over and over again how good I make you feel. Understood?"

"Yes, Sir," she responds as her head rolls along my shoulder.

Reaching around her, I grab a bundle of hemp and drag the soft rope along her skin as I loop it under and over her heaving breasts. With the loops both secure, I kiss along her shoulders as I braid the strands of rope over her shoulders and secure them to the loops circling her torso. I delicately pull both of her arms behind her back and position her so that she is holding both of her elbows. Weaving the hemp around her arms and binding them in place, I praise her, "Such a good little rope bunny for me."

With the final knot in place, I lower her to the floor and rest her on her side so I can work the second bundle of rope around her leg more easily. Placing a double-column knot above and below her knee, I cinch it tightly before standing. The third bundle of hemp runs through the suspension brackets and pulls on the ropes meticulously tied around Quinn. I give a few pulls at the rope, and she gasps as she suddenly finds herself partially suspended in her harnesses as she tries to steady herself on the tippy toes of her right foot.

Undoing the hair elastic, her long red locks cascade toward the ground. I push them out of her face and let them fall over her shoulder. My fingers run over her skin and braids of rope, following the dip of her waist and the curvature of her hips as I bend between her parted thighs. "My little rope bunny is dripping." I run my tongue through her glistening slit and suck it into my mouth with a groan. "And it tastes too fucking good not to lick it all from you."

Gripping her hips with both hands, I pull her toward my mouth and kiss her swollen mound. I lick and suck at her until her tight clit throbs against my tongue. She cries out a blissful scream, her flexed leg trembling, as I take her over the edge.

"I would stop," I groan against her, "but you taste too fucking good, and I want you coming on my tongue again."

My cock tents my pants, growing ever more rigid from eating between Quinn's thighs. I can't get enough of her pussy on my tongue and the way her sweet tang coats my mouth. Lapping at her like a starved man, I fucking love the power it gives me. She's helpless when I make her legs—and her whole body—quiver from the mere flick of my tongue. But I am fucking addicted to the sounds she makes and the flood of arousal that gushes into my mouth when I suck at her clit and cause her to violently come undone.

I swirl the tip of my tongue around her clit and pull it into my mouth. Tugging and suckling at it, I grind it against my tongue as Quinn writhes in the ropes. She screams out my name, and I swallow every drop of her sweet spray as my cock throbs against my zipper.

CHAPTER THIRTY-TWO

QUINN

"Stick out your tongue," Declan demands as his fingers slide into my hair and he bends to my level. My arousal shines on his lips, and the glistening liquid drips from his chin. Inching his face toward mine, he gravelly commands, "Clean up your mess."

My pussy somehow flutters again as I lick along the underside of his jaw, collecting a drop of me. I follow it with wet, suckling kisses over his chin, moaning as I lick my arousal from his face. Tightening his grip on the fistful of my hair, Declan pulls me to his mouth and plunges his tongue into mine. He rubs his tongue against mine, painting it with my taste, kissing me hard until I'm left panting and breathless.

"Such a dirty girl," he groans, pulling back from our kiss and standing. He disappears behind me, his hands gliding over my body tell me where he's going. They slide along my leg, which is poised on the floor, until they're lightly wrapped around my ankle. He places a ticklish kiss behind my knee as he lifts my foot from the floor. Bending it toward my ass, he holds it in place and secures it with a length of hemp, leaving me fully suspended.

And totally at his mercy.

Mercy that he immediately takes advantage of when he spreads my thighs, slips the head of the pink wand through my arousal and presses it against my clit. His hand slides over my hip and splays across my stomach to hold me flush against his body. His firm cock presses into the small of my back as he flips the vibrator on.

"Fuck! Dec!" I scream and lurch in my ropes as the brutally strong vibrations shoot through me, but he doesn't turn it down. Pained whimpers tremble over my lips as he grinds the head of the wand over my clit at varying levels of pressure. Mere moments of relief mixed with blissful agony.

"You can take a little more," Declan groans as I spasm violently against him from the string of orgasms rushing through my body. His hand slides along my stomach until it is cupping my breast. He kneads it and teasingly pulls at my nipples as he continues to hold the vibe firmly between my legs. "I'm not stopping until you've left a puddle on this floor. I want to watch as you completely let go."

I struggle, literally and figuratively, through every orgasm, with our safe word resting on the tip of my tongue. While I come more times than I can count,

Declan continues to massage the wand on and around my clit. Another orgasm rapidly builds at my core until my pussy feels like it's going to explode. The release shoots through me, gushing from my pussy and expelling from my mouth in a silent scream.

"You did so fucking good for me, *mo chéadsearc*," Declan praises, flipping off the wand and ending the incessant buzzing. A euphoric calmness wafts over me as he tenderly rubs his hands over my skin and continues to shower me with praise.

"I love how fucking wet you get for me," Declan croons. Undoing his pants, he steps between my parted thighs and presses the thick head of his cock into me. He thrusts into me at a leisurely pace, keeping a soft grip on my leg and the harness around my chest to stabilize me. "I'm getting fucking covered in you."

I lose all track of time, and it feels like Declan worships me for hours as rolling waves of pleasure continue to ripple through me. Declan grows more rigid inside me, causing me to quiver around him as it catapults me over the edge again. My pussy squeezes around him, and it's his undoing. He slides in deep, his hips pressing against me as he groans through his release. Pulling from me, he mutters, "I might never get enough of filling you."

My eyelids grow heavy as Declan pulls and tugs at the ropes, jostling me slightly. Opening them, I find myself on the floor even though my body still feels weightless. I'm sitting between Declan's legs, propped against his chest, as he pulls the last of the ropes from around my legs. My skin is pink and dimpled with the spiral pattern from the ropes.

"You did so good for me. I'm so fucking proud of you." Declan tenderly rubs his fingers over the marks as he languidly kisses along my neck. He spreads his hand over my flat stomach and tips my face over my shoulder to face him. His warm breath blows across my lips as he leans close to delicately press his to them.

Lifting me from the floor, Declan carries me across the room and slides us both into the bed. He curls against my back, spooning me. His arms wrap around me and pull me against him. "I don't want to wait," he whispers, and I try desperately to fight off my exhaustion. "I want you as my wife. I want to start building a life with you."

Sliding my hands along his forearm, I pull his hand to my lips and kiss the back of it. "I'd marry you tomorrow. But we've already started building a life together, baby."

CHAPTER THIRTY-THREE
DECLAN

The sun is just beginning to creep over the horizon as I wake. When I slide from bed, I pull the covers over Quinn's naked body and place a soft kiss on her forehead before heading down the hall. I pause at Fiona's room to crack the door, finding her still fast asleep. It inadvertently clicks when I pull it shut, resulting in a groggy, "*Daidí?*"

"Yes, *a stóirín*. It's just me," I let myself back into her room and take a seat on the bed. She crawls from under the covers and into my lap as we talk about this being her new room and the exciting new life we're all going to have in our new home.

"Will Quinn be my *mammy*?" I'm left with a lump in my throat as her innocent question leaves me without an answer.

"No, kiddo," Quinn softly answers, and I turn to find her wrapped in her robe and watching the two of us from the doorway. She sits beside me on the bed and rests her head on my shoulder as her hand rubs over Fiona's back. "I could never replace your *mammy*, but I will love you just as much as she does."

"She loves me a lot," Fiona shares. "*Daidi* tells me all the time how much she loves me."

Nothing like having your three-year-old tear your heart out before sunrise.

"She sure does," Quinn agrees. She pulls Fiona from my lap and onto hers, breaking the heaviness of the room. With a playful smile, Quinn squeezes her tightly, energetically exclaiming, "And I love you this much."

Fiona squeaks, letting out a barrage of giggles when Quinn tickles along her back. Pushing her away, she impishly huffs, "You love me too much."

"Never, kiddo." Quinn smiles as she shakes her head. She grabs my hand and squeezes it tightly when she stands from the bed. "I think we should make your dad show us around this new big house, because I heard something about a pool."

"A pool!" Fiona exclaims, grabbing my other hand and using her entire body weight as she attempts to pull me from the bed.

Leaning toward Quinn, I place a kiss on her shoulder and whisper, "I love you, *mo chéadsearc,*" before pretending Fiona drags me to my feet.

"Breakfast first, *a stóirín*," I swoop Fiona into my arms and carry her downstairs as Quinn follows behind us. Fiona wiggles from my hold when we reach the landing, eager to check out all the new toys in the living room. We leave her to play while getting something together for breakfast. Stepping into the kitchen, I'm surprised to find Conor and Liam sitting at the island.

"Good morning," Conor greets us. A smirk spreads across his face, and he teases, "But I'm assuming not quite as good as last night."

Quinn grabs the dishtowel on the counter and rightfully tosses it at him.

"I'm all for christening your new place, but the two of you know it's common manners to greet guests when they come to your house, right?" Liam further harasses the two of us. "That it's a little rude to make them let themselves in."

"Shit!" Finn exclaims as he walks into our conversation. "You weren't the ones that walked in here first. I ran upstairs thinking the two of them were getting murdered, not that he was fucking slaying her pussy."

The lot of them roar in laughter as Tristan and Layla join us all in the kitchen, and he razzes Finn. "You're one to talk. We had the *pleasure* of listening to you fuck your hand for at least an hour."

"One, it wasn't my hand," Finn imparts. "Two, listening to her made me hard as fucking hell."

"Did you fucking whack off to my wife?" I snarl, a mixture of faux and real anger, as I storm around the counter to put the little shit in a headlock.

"No. I whacked off to Scarlett Johanson." he chokes, and I release my hold on him. He shoves me away, darting around the island as he snarks. "She just sounds a fucking lot like Quinn."

"I'm going to fucking kill him," I grit through my teeth. Laughing hard, Quinn shoves her hands against my chest to stop me from chasing after him. "Don't fucking encourage him," I huff, gripping her wrists and looking down at her.

Quinn condescendingly pats her hands against my chest. "It's too early in the morning to murder him, and I'd hate to be scrubbing his blood out of the cracks of these brand-new floors."

"You should listen to her," Finn scoffs.

"Am I the only one of you lot that heard him call her 'his wife'?" Tristan asks, eyeing the two of us inquisitively.

All eyes turn to us, eagerly awaiting an answer. I stare down at Quinn and stroke my knuckles along her jaw. "She's not yet, but she's going to be soon." Quinn beams up at me before pressing onto her toes and placing a kiss on my cheek.

"You knocked her up, didn't you?" Finn jests.

Falling back onto her heels, Quinn slides her hands from my chest. She steps out from in front of me and gestures toward Finn mock-angrily. "Now you can fucking kill him."

CHAPTER THIRTY-FOUR

QUINN

After receiving a plethora of welcoming and congratulatory hugs from all of Declan's brothers—even a slightly battered Finn—the boys all retreated to the patio at the back of the house. Layla and I are making breakfast as Fiona lies on the floor in the next room, coloring.

Less than twelve hours in this house, and it already feels like a home.

"How soon are you looking to marry that bunch?" Layla asks as she glances out the windows overlooking the patio to where all the boys are sitting. They surround the fire pit as they take a call with Rory, the serious expressions on their faces making it obvious that he didn't call with good news.

Layla's question may raise some eyebrows—*actually a lot of eyebrows and outlandish gasps*—to an outsider, but I know exactly what she means. Marrying into this family doesn't give you a brother-in-law—like most brides gain. Nothing more than a new family member that you communicate with casually and at family gatherings. Joining this family gives you five men who will not only love and cherish you but will also sacrifice their lives to save yours. Because all of them would do absolutely anything for their family.

Yet, my curiosity is piqued.

"You don't still..." I hesitate, trying to find the appropriate words to tactfully ask my question. Failing, I blurt, "You know...Conor."

"No. It was just that once." She shakes her head. "I was curious, so Tristan let me experience it."

"And things aren't weird?"

"Other than knowing Conor's pierced cock is equally impressive as Tristan's, and I now can't help but imagine all of them to be? No."

And just like that, I'm pretty sure I will never not think about Conor's piercing when I see him.

"Why do you ask? Are you looking to see what it's like being shared by two of them?"

"God, no!" I exclaim.

Tristan clears his throat, and we both look up to find all five of them standing in the archway to the kitchen. There is no controlling the heated flush that rushes up my neck and over my cheeks.

"What?" Layla shrugs, pausing for a moment to glance into the next room to ensure Fiona is still occupied with her toys and not our conversation., before doubling down. "She's fucking hot, and every last one of you would be more than eager to fuck her."

"I would," Finn eagerly blurts, raising his hand. His admission immediately draws a growl-filled glare from Declan.

"I am absolutely not interested in fucking any of you," I vehemently declare as Declan crosses the room to me.

"Good." He wraps his arms around me and pulls me possessively tightly as his teeth sink into the crook of my neck with enough force that I yelp. He kisses over the mark he left, his tongue caressing it to soothe the sharp pain. With his lips still pressed to my skin, his words vibrate against me when he says, "Because I'm a possessive fuck. I don't share my wife, not even with my brothers."

Conor taunts, "I mean, technically, she's not your wife yet."

"He isn't wrong," I tease, immediately regretting the words when Declan nips at my neck again.

"We're going to rectify that," he growls. "I'll make a call, and we can be married on the beach by the end of the night."

"Declan Cathal Evans," I admonish, causing his brothers to snicker at the use of his full name. Snapping around in my chair. "Your *mam* would roll over in her grave over you even contemplating getting married anywhere but inside a church. And being that this is the only time I am getting married, I would prefer it not be on our backyard beach in shorts solely so your brothers can't fuck me."

"I don't appreciate the sass, *mo chéadsearc*. I'll let it slide because I can't argue. *Mam* would come back from the grave to haunt me, and you do deserve the wedding you've always desired. You can have whatever you want as long as you plan it by Saturday." Gripping my chin, he places a kiss against my lips. When he pulls back, he doesn't relinquish his hold as he speaks against my ear, the volume just loud enough that everyone else can hear him. "I'll wait, but know that I'm going to spend the next three days thoroughly reminding you that you are mine. And only fucking mine."

I've always known that Declan was overly protective, but as he breathes his words against my ear, I see just how deep his jealousy runs. He's possessive as hell, and I like it.

No…I fucking love it.

My pussy flutters, and my panties are getting damper with every passing word of his promise—*or is it a threat?*—as he continues to whisper, "Not a minute will pass that you aren't full of my cock or dripping my cum out of that tight little cunt nestled between your thighs. Understood?"

A gulp bobs in my throat before quietly answering, "Yes, Sir."

"Good girl," he whispers as his lips slide along my cheek until they find their destination, and he leaves a soft, feathery kiss that lingers on my lips.

"Is anyone else fucking hard?" Finn whispers to Conor and Liam beside him, causing me to snicker.

"Liam and I have to go meet Rory about the apartment soon," Declan informs me as he refills my glass of juice and slides it before me. Hovering over me, he demands, "Drink up. You're going to need it because I'm fucking two loads of cum into you before I leave."

"Really?" Finn adjusts himself. "Just me?"

CHAPTER THIRTY-FIVE
DECLAN

As much as I don't want to leave Quinn and Fiona right now, I know they will be safe with Tristan, Conor, and Finn. Liam came with me because, unlike me, he understands all this tech shit.

"They haven't just been watching, though. They've been looping the feed," Rory informs us both.

"Looping the what?" I ask, clearly the only one who doesn't understand what Rory is saying.

"They record clips from the feed, such as empty elevators or people sleeping, then basically play it back through our monitors," Liam educates me.

"Right," Rory confirms. "Then, while we're watching the recording of a vacant stairwell or Miss Fiona sleeping, they're able to move about the building and your apartment freely because we can't see them."

"How long?" I demand, trying to stow my anger.

Rory hesitates before answering. "About two and half months."

"Two and a half fucking months!" I seethe.

"We're still kind of guessing here, Declan," Rory admits. "We've been tracing it back, and so far, that's the furthest back we've found discrepancies in the timestamps on the recorded footage."

"How?" I snarl.

I pace through the living room of my abandoned apartment as I continue to listen to Rory. "We haven't figured that out yet. There is no evidence of a hack, not a single security breach."

"Not a single security breach?" I scoff his words back at him before yelling. "Someone has been watching my family for months. A man has been creeping around my house and watching my daughter sleep. And you're going to tell me that there hasn't been a fucking security breach?"

Liam interrupts me to ask Rory, "And you're relatively sure that it's only been two and a half months?"

"The best we can be for now," Rory responds with uncertainty in his tone.

Abruptly turning his attention back to me, Liam asks, "When did Quinn move in?"

"You aren't fucking suggesting—"

"No, absolutely not," Liam cuts me off before I can finish, shaking his head. "I'm suggesting that maybe this has absolutely nothing to do with you or our war with the Bratva. And that maybe it has *everything* to do with Quinn."

I continue to pace anxiously along windows overlooking the terrace, waiting for Liam to get to his point. "For fuck's sake, just spit it out then."

"It's Quinn," Liam exclaims. "They might be threatening all three of you, but they're watching Quinn."

Quinn...

They're planning. Plotting. Learning my weaknesses and our schedules. Patiently watching as they wait for the opportune moment. The moment they can take her.

She's what they want.

"They want their vengeance—"

"On us both," I interrupt Liam. "Killing her, or whatever they plan to do with her, isn't just about the lone man she killed in the bar. They knew from the moment Tris and I killed the other two from that night. I practically took out a billboard in Times Square, letting them know she was important to me. They'll destroy her because they know what it'll do to me."

"Bringing her on as your nanny likely has kept her safe," Rory imparts. "We had guys watching her, but the security at her place was nothing compared to here. Moving her made her harder to get to.”

“He's right,” Liam agrees. “Even having access to the security footage, it took them the entire time she's been here to actually make a play for her.”

“And,” Rory grows more excitable, “she had to have been the initial target. The fixation on Miss Fiona started after. About the same time you killed Akim.”

“But why now?” I ask rhetorically. “Why make a move now?”

“They've managed to sneak a single man in and out of here for weeks without us knowing. But it was only ever just a single man, and he was never brazen enough to make contact,” Rory shares.

“Managing to avert the security feed is one thing. Dragging a screaming woman and child past numerous armed guards unnoticed is another,” Liam imparts.

“So, what changed?” I ask them both.

The three of us ponder for a moment, with Rory being the first of us to break the silence, “They either found a way to get Quinn and Fiona out of here—”

I cut him off, “Or they wanted us to go somewhere else.”

Pulling my phone from my pocket, I send a quick group text to my brothers.

Be on alert.

The Bratva might have the upper hand, and it might not be today, but they ARE coming for Quinn and Fiona.

TRISTAN

Quinn and Fiona are safe here with us

FINN

You know we'll keep them safe

CONOR

Like they're our own

We're heading back now.

You better.

I know they will. It's no longer just about the five of us. All of them would lay down their life to protect Quinn and Fiona, just like I would for Layla.

Rud ar bith do mo theaghlach.

CHAPTER THIRTY-SIX
QUINN

Everyone's phones lit up about thirty minutes ago, and while I can't quite put my finger on it, but suddenly, something is different about the boys.

Something is happening.

Declan walks through the front door with Liam and Rory on his heel. "Liam will get you all up to speed," he says to his brothers as he passes. "Layla, can you please keep an eye on Fiona?"

"I need you upstairs," he barks before grabbing my hand and pulling me up the stairs.

"Oh my God. It's barely been an hour since you were inside of me," I dramatically exclaim. The only acknowledgment I receive from him is a disapproving glance over his shoulder as he squeezes my hand harder and continues dragging me toward our bedroom. He closes the door, and I continue to brat, "And trust me, you're still dripping from me too."

"I love you, *mo chéadsearc*, but right now, I need you to shut up and listen to what I tell you."

"Dec," my voice catches, "you're scaring me."

"Good," he huffs, "because you need to be." Using his hold on my hand, he pulls me into him. His arms wrap around me, completely enveloping me in his embrace, and he squeezes me painfully tightly. His lips dust over my forehead as he releases me. The touch of his hand doesn't leave me as he leads me to the couch.

"Before I tell you anything, I need you to know that I will protect you with my life. All of us will. Do you understand?"

I nod my response. Remembering Declan doesn't like when I don't use my words, I blurt, "Yes, Sir."

"The cameras. They didn't start watching until you moved in. They were watching you."

"Me?" My brows scrunch. "All over one greasy guy at the bar that even his friends didn't bother to stop and mourn."

"Yes and no." Declan pulls me onto his lap so he can hold me closer. "We think they want you for the guy in the bar, but they also want you for what I did to the two other guys. They know that taking you—or Fiona— will hurt me more than anything they could do to me."

He continues to tell me everything they've learned, including how taking this job with him likely saved my life.

In more ways than one, apparently.

"They made a move because they *could*. Something changed, and they know how to get their hands on you." He cups my face and stares into my eyes as he assures me, "I have no intentions of leaving your side. No one will ever hurt you again, *mo chéadsearc*."

"Promise?" I choke, fighting back the tears. While I know he will do anything to protect me, I am terrified when I imagine what will happen to me if the Bratva ever get their hands on me. Death would be better than any nightmarish scenario I've dreamed up. Better than everything I've already survived.

"One that I will die for to ensure I never break it again." Declan pulls my face the short distance toward his. His lips vibrate against mine when he speaks again. "I won't lose you again."

I don't know if it's his unwavering commitment to protecting me or the overwhelming fear of death, but I find myself needing him. Licking along the seam of his lips, I press my tongue into his mouth. He doesn't hesitate to pull me tighter and kiss me back. The kiss is long and deep, and I find myself grinding against his lap as I whimper into his mouth with need.

"Fuck, you make it impossible to keep my hands off you," Declan speaks through our kiss

"Then don't."

Wrapping his hands around my waist, Declan twists and pins me to the couch beneath him. He kisses along my neck as his hips circle, grinding his already hard length against me. Lifting slightly, he rolls me beneath him until I'm on my stomach, immediately returning his lips to my neck.

"I can't deny my needy little *wife*," he whispers along my neck, "but we need to be fast so we can get back downstairs."

With Declan straddling my legs, my heart races with anticipation as I listen to him undo his zipper. He grips the waistline of my pants and roughly yanks them over my ass before using them to tug it into the air.

Declan presses the entirety of himself into me with a single stroke, and I groan in both pleasure and the discomfort of him stretching me so quickly. He uses the grip on my pants for leverage to slam into me hard and fast, leaving me grunting and biting the seat cushion beneath me to keep from screaming out in pleasure as he drives me toward my release.

Grabbing my hands, he pulls them both over my head, leans over me, and presses me to the couch beneath the weight of his body. His hot, panting breath blows against my neck as he buries his face in the crook of my neck. "Bite that fucking pillow because I haven't even begun to fuck you hard yet."

He thrusts into me at an ungodly speed, his thick cock hitting every last spot that I need him to. The orgasm he's building swells at my core, and I bury my face into the couch, using it to muffle my screams as I violently come undone beneath him. Withdrawing nearly from me, he slams into me again and moans through the pleasure of his release against my shoulder.

Pulling himself from me, he groans as he runs his finger along my pussy, collecting his cum. "That sweet little pussy of yours is so fucking full that I'm dripping from you."

He rubs it along my entrance to press it back into me and pulls my pants back over my ass as I struggle to catch my breath. "Thank you, Sir," I pant. "Because fucking a baby into me is the other promise I'm expecting you to keep."

CHAPTER THIRTY-SEVEN
DECLAN

Quinn is about to open the door when I stop her and pull her back against my chest. Sliding my hand up her body, I lightly wrap my fingers around her throat and angle her face toward mine. "Plan our wedding, *mo chéadsearc*. I don't care what is happening; what the threats are. I'm not going to let the Bratva keep us apart."

We've already lost over a decade of a life we could have had together. Losing more time seems frivolous. I want to finally do right by her and give her the life that she's always wanted. The one she's always deserved. The one I threw away trying to protect her when, ironically, not being mine nearly cost her life.

"Good." She leans back into my chest and smirks. "The Catholic girl in me would really like to be married before you knock me up."

From the tone of her voice, I can tell that she is only partially joking.

"Is that the same good little Catholic girl that just thanked me for filling her tight little cunt as I fucked her from behind so hard that she had to muffle her screams?" I tease. "Or are you referring to the good little Catholic girl that had her hands tied to the headboard with her bound ankles on my shoulders this morning?"

"You know what I mean!" she huffs exasperatedly.

I continue to toy with her, "You're right. You screamed God's name so much this morning; he probably counted it as your penance and already forgave you for your sins."

"You are absolutely fucking incorrigible." She shakes her head and pulls the door open.

"You love it," I quip. "There is one thing that I am deadly serious about, though. I am marrying you by this weekend."

"We will never be able to secure the church on such short notice," Quinn argues as we make our way back downstairs.

"You let me worry about that," I request as we rejoin everyone, finding them all gathered around the large kitchen island. "I'll send Finn to talk to Father O'Flaherty and make it happen."

"That man hates me," Finn interjects himself into our conversation.

"He's a priest!" Liam exclaims. "His entire life is built on the premise of helping people atone for their sins and fucking forgiveness. He doesn't *hate* anyone."

"Well, I think then he maybe holds a grudge over the number of times I've caused him to drop his bible in the confessional." Finn shrugs.

"Sure." Tristan condescendingly pats him on the back. "I'm sure that's what it is. It probably has nothing to do with when you were fifteen, and you fingered Missy O'Harrah to completion in the middle of Sunday mass."

"Maybe don't send Finn." Quinn rolls her eyes at Finn as she laughs.

"You make a few girls come in church, and this is the..." Finn sighs.

"A *few*?" I scoff. "This is like the strippers all over again. I want to know. But I also don't want to."

"It's the tartan skirts," Finn shares without waiting for me to ask. "And after Missy, I didn't exactly have a shortage of options."

I merely shake my head.

I knew I didn't want to know.

"I'll go," Liam volunteers, then points at Tristan and Conor. "And I'll take whichever one of you two Father O'Flaherty hasn't caught with your fingers or cock inside of a member of his congregation."

"Take Tristan," Conor flatly insists.

"For fuck's sake!" I exclaim. "You too?"

"In my defense, it was the courtyard *behind* the church." Conor loses his ability to maintain his straight face and snickers. "Because those fucking plaid skirts."

"And you're worried about *mam* rolling over in her grave because of me?" I look at Quinn.

"She smacked the shit out of us both," Finn shares as he laughs. "And she would've smacked the shit out of you, too."

This fucking family.

"Tris. Liam. Can you please take care of the church?" I ask when the laughter and jokes finally subside. They both nod and collectively gather their things to take care of this favor for me. "Conor and Finn can help me and Rory with some security deficits around here before it gets dark."

"And me?" Quinn chimes in.

"You, *mo chéadsearc, you* get to have Layla help you pull together your dream wedding," I respond, pulling out my wallet and retrieving a credit card for her. "Use my office. Let me know anything the two of you can't do from there, and we'll take care of it."

The girls disappear to my office with Fiona while I head outside with Conor, Finn, and Rory to look for even the slightest infrastructure weakness *we* would exploit if needed to get on the property. We walk the perimeter.

"This is a great property from a security standpoint," Rory acknowledges. "The waterfront completely removes a fast access point, and the yard is vast enough that we should see anyone coming that makes it past the perimeter."

"Not should." My tone is gruff. "I want the men positioned so they can take out anyone who makes it more than two feet past the fence."

"Understood."

Trying to find Akim's son has gone about as well as figuring out where the Pakhan has been hiding out all these months. Both of them are like ghosts. *Invisible.* Each of them make rare appearances when they have a reason to reach out. There isn't too much more we can really do.

Except wait.

Sitting here waiting for someone to come and take Quinn from me is torturous. The only other time in my life I've felt this helpless was when I had to watch Sarah die.

CHAPTER THIRTY-EIGHT

QUINN

Two days later...

"Out!" I demand, shoving Declan toward the door.

Staring down at me with sad, puppy eyes, he grovels, "*Mo chéadsearc.*"

"I'm serious, Dec," I huff, trying desperately to stay strong. "It's bad luck to see the bride before the wedding. And that means you aren't sleeping here.

A smug smirk pulls at the corner of his lips as he forces himself back into the room, slamming the door behind him, as he growls, "No one said *anything* about sleeping."

Before I have another chance to rebut, his lips are on mine, and his tongue is pressing into my mouth. Kissing me hard and deep, his hands slide along my back until they're on my thighs. He gives a firm tug, lifting me from the ground. My legs instinctually wrap around him as he drives me into the wall.

Pinned between him and the wall, I groan his name through our kiss, "Dec…"

Pulling his lips from mine, he breathes warm kisses along my neck, sucking tenderly between them until I'm a whimpering mess. His words vibrate against my skin as he groans, "I'll give you what you want. I won't stay."

He gently lowers my feet to the ground and places a soft kiss against my lips. Another under my chin. It's followed by a trail of kisses over my shirt as he takes his time kneeling before me. Staring up my body, he undoes the button to my jeans and lowers the zipper, gravelly whispering, "But first, you're going to let me show you just how much I'm looking forward to taking you as *my wife*."

Declan rids me of my pants and panties as he nibbles and kisses over the lips of my pussy. "Do you want me to show you?"

"Yes, Sir," I moan my response when he dips his tongue through my lips and against my clit.

His fingers dust along the back of my leg, tickling behind my knee and sliding over the sensitive skin, as he pulls my leg over his shoulder. Spread wide and hovering over his face, he places a long, slow lick of his tongue. "I can still taste all the babies I put in you this morning."

Fuck, that's hot.

I swirl my hips and grind against his tongue, desperately

needing more. He continues to tease and suck, knowing exactly how to hold me at the edge.

"You love knowing that my cum coats every inch of your cunt, don't you?" he asks, momentarily replacing his tongue with his thumb.

I groan as the pad rubs firmly over the sensitive bundle of nerves before responding, "Yes, Sir."

"You want more of it, don't you? So much of it that I'll be dripping down your legs as you walk down the aisle tomorrow."

My hips spasm as he holds me on the brink. "Please, Sir," I plead.

Smiling broadly at my answer, Declan pulls my other leg over his shoulders, leaving me sitting on him with my back pressed to the windows behind me. "Be a good girl and show me how much. Put that pink pussy on my tongue and ride my face as you beg. I want to hear how badly you want it as you come undone."

He cups my ass to help support my weight, staring up at me as he waits for me to follow his instructions. Arching my back, I push myself over his face, and the first touch of his tongue on my skin nearly does me in. Rocking my hips, I ride his mouth as his tongue licks through me, panting. "You're going to make me come."

His tongue licks firmly over my clit, increasing in speed as I ride him harder until I'm trembling on his tongue, and I cry out when my release shoots through me. "Your tongue feels so fucking good," I moan as I come down. Sliding my fingers into his hair, I stare down at his arousal-coated face as he stares up my body, hanging on my every word. "Your tongue makes me so fucking wet. Making my pussy drip so I can take your thick cock."

The intimacy of staring into his eyes as I ride his face has me on the precipice. When he moans at my words, and the vibrations pulse over my clit, I'm done for. My thighs squeeze against his face as he continues to swirl his tongue around my clit.

"Sir," I scream before begging like he asked of me. *Begging for exactly what I want.* "Please, Sir. I want your cock in me. Fucking me. I want it. Sir, please fuck me until you're coming in my pussy."

Declan growls against my pussy, lapping at me hungrily as his hands roughly palm my ass. Feasting on me and denying my pleas to fuck me as he repeatedly forces me to come again and again on his tongue. My desire to have him inside me grows with every plead until it's no longer a want. It's a need.

"I need your cock." The words sound pained as they tremble over my lips. "I need you to fuck me. Fuck me full of your cum until you put babies in me."

Sliding me off his shoulders, Declan pulls me down to his lap and his awaiting rock-hard cock. He drags me over it, and the feel of him sliding inside me sends quivers through my entire body.

"Such a good girl for me," Declan praises as his lips dust over mine. "Begging me to give you what you want."

CHAPTER THIRTY-NINE
DECLAN

I lift us both from the floor and carry Quinn to our bed, keeping my cock buried deep inside her. With one hand, I hold her against me and, I pull her shirt over her head with the other. She melts into the bed when I lay her upon it. Thrusting into her at a slow, leisurely pace, I kiss over her neck and pert tits as my hands roam along her body and hold her legs over my hip. She hovers on the brink, her hips rising to meet mine as she desperately tries to take more of me.

"Do you want it deeper?" I ask, inching my cock into her until I'm buried to the hilt. I still for a moment before pulling out and slamming my hips against her ass. "Or do you want it harder?"

"Both," she answers timidly. "Can I have both, Sir?"

Fuck, I couldn't say no if I tried.

"Yes, good girl for asking for what you need." I cup her chin and place a chaste kiss against her lips. Pulling my cock from her, I climb from the bed, instructing, "Up by the headboard for me."

Leaving her for a moment as I cross the room, she slides her tired body toward the top of the bed. I grab what I need from the armoire—a telescopic spreader bar, cuffs, and two short sections of hemp rope—and my cock throbs at the thought of how good she's going to look. After I drop the items on the bed, I strip out of my clothes and toss them to the floor.

"Fuck, my wife is beautiful."

I climb onto the bed and prowl across it, until I reach Quinn, positioning her on the pillows until she is in an almost crunch. My lips travel the length of her left arm, starting at her shoulder. Reaching her wrist, I wrap the cuff around it. I do the same to the right before kissing down her body to her toes. Dragging the velvet interior of the leather cuffs along her legs, I wrap each one around her ankles and attach them to the spreader bar.

"You're being so patient," I praise, tying a clove hitch around the spreader bar at each of her ankles. Reaching over her, I loop the loose ends of the hemp around the iron slats at each side of the headboard. I slowly tighten the slack on the ropes, lifting her legs into the air as the telescopic bar inches wider. When I secure the loose ends of the hemp around the bar, Quinn's legs are in a deep V, with her toes pointed toward the headboard. "Fuck. You look so good spread open for me with that dripping pussy of yours on display."

I lean between her legs, licking along the length of her pussy and across the cheek of her ass. My lips and tongue leave a trail of wet kisses up the back of her right leg as I take my time securing her right wrist to the bar. Kissing down her arm and across her chest, I clip her other wrist to the bar. The tightly bound position leaves her staring down her body. "Can you see your glistening cunt?"

"Yes, Sir." She nods before looking up at me.

"Good"—I direct her eyes back between her thighs—"because I want you to watch every stroke of my cock. I want you to watch me pump every last drop cum into your soaking wet cunt. Would you like that? Watching as I put our baby in you?"

Quinn's pussy spasms as I slide the tip of my cock along her slit, waiting for her answer. "Yes! Please, Sir."

"Your tight little cunt feels so fucking good when you slide over me," I groan, pressing into her at a pace that is torturously slow for us both. She feels so fucking good that it takes every bit of self-restraint to keep from plowing into her. "Watch me stretch you out. I want you to see how eager your pussy is for my cock."

Fully seated inside her, I rock my hips and relish in the tight warmth of her cunt wrapped around me. Her arousal coats my shaft and trickles down her ass, dampening the sheets beneath us, as I continue to thrust in and out of her. She quivers around my cock as her legs flex in their tight bindings, a breathy moan passing over her lips as she comes.

"Fuck, I love how you feel when you come."

Rubbing my thumb lightly over her clit, I bring her over the edge again. And again. Every orgasm building stronger than the last as she slowly works me to my release.

But it's not enough.

"I need to fuck you, *mo chéadsearc*," I grit. "I want you screaming and clenching around me when I fill this tight little hole."

She glances up at me through her thick lashes. Her lust-fueled need is more than enough of an answer, and without waiting for her to speak, I drive into her. Driving hard and fast, her already tight cunt begins to squeeze relentlessly around my cock as she rides a string of never-ending orgasms.

"Open. Your. Eyes," I grunt through thrusts as she struggles through her explosive release. "Watch me...give you...what...you're begging...for." My cock twitches as she squeezes blissfully around me, milking my cock as I unload in her until our cum begins to trickle from her. I pull from her slowly, ensuring every bit of my release stays inside of her. Removing her cuffs one at a time, I pepper the skin with soft kisses before laying each of her tired limbs on the bed.

Crawling beside her, I pull her into me and kiss over her neck and the back of her shoulder. "I love you, Dec," she mutters groggily.

"I love you, *mo chéadsearc.*"" I whisper against her ear.

She stirs slightly and mumbles, "You can't." Her words are so slow and heavy as she clearly fights against exhaustion.

"Don't worry," I kiss at the crook of her shoulder, "I'm only staying until you fall asleep. The next time I see you, you'll be walking toward me at the altar. Making me the happiest man alive."

CHAPTER FORTY

QUINN

I can't believe this is happening...

I spent years of my life dreaming about marrying Declan and becoming Mrs. Quinn Evans. The path we took to get here was tumultuous and full of heartache, but we're here. It looks different from what I had imagined—*a ready-made family*—but I wouldn't trade that little girl for anything.

"Quinn?" Tristan knocks on the door and cracks it slightly. "Are you decent? Or am I going to get an eyeful when I come in?"

"You're just going to have to take your chances," I chuckle.

"*Tá tú go hálainn*," Tristan marvels as he enters the room. "Absolutely beautiful, Mrs. Evans. I've never seen you happier."

"Stop," I sniffle, rapidly blinking to hold back the tears as Tristan closes the distance between us. "You're going to make me cry, and this makeup took forever."

"I wouldn't want to do that." He gives me a tender hug and kisses my forehead. "I'm taking Layla, Fiona, and Declan to the church. Conor, Finn, and Rory are waiting for you downstairs."

"Is the armed convoy really necessary?" I huff.

"It's the only way he's willing to let you out of his sight." Tristan places a soft kiss on my cheek. "We'll see you at the church, beautiful."

"Let them know I'll be ready in about five minutes," I call to Tristan as he walks toward the door.

Standing before the mirror, I glance at my appearance while I wait for Declan to leave the house. Having such little time to pull this together, I am still in awe of the dress Layla found. It's classic and modest, with a full tulle skirt that makes me feel like a princess. The spaghetti-strapped lace bodice ties at the back, making it fit like a glove without needing to deal with the hassle of fittings and alterations, even if we'd had time.

It's the perfect finishing touch for this fairytale.

I garner Finn's attention first. His eyes rake over my body as I walk down the stairs, and he exclaims, "You're a right *feek*!"

"Too fucking beautiful for Declan. But you always were," Conor croons, taking my hand at the landing. He pulls me close, places a kiss against my cheek, and whispers. "And too good for him. Too good for all of us."

"I love you too, Conor," I kiss his cheek.

"This is fucking bullshit," Finn teasingly huffs. "First Layla, now Quinn. You'll probably wind up scoring Liam's girl, too."

Slipping from Conor's light embrace, I step closer to Finn. I stand on my tippy-toes and place a chaste kiss at the corner of his lips. "And I love you too, Finnigan."

Arm in arm with both of them, they walk me to the two SUVs waiting in the driveway. "You're going to ride with Rory," Conor informs me. "Finn and I will be in the SUV behind you to watch the cars around you."

"You look beautiful," Rory shares as he helps me into the backseat of the Suburban. The three of them ensure my fluffy dress is tucked into the car before shutting the door. Rory climbs into the driver's seat and pulls to the gate before stopping to wait for the boys. When they approach behind us, he pushes the button to open the gate and merges into traffic.

Uncharacteristically, Rory makes casual small talk with me as we drive. While he's still a little curt and rough around the edges, it's nice. I also think I've learned more about him in the past fifteen minutes than I have in the months I've spent with him as my bodyguard.

"Shit!" Rory exclaims, his eyes darting between the rearview mirror and the road before us as he drastically decreases his speed. Craning my neck to look over the backseat, I see a garbage truck parked in the side of Conor and Finn's crumpled SUV.

"Stop, Rory!" I gasp. "Conor and Finn!"

Instead of braking, Rory stomps on the gas. I watch the odometer climb as he weaves in and out of traffic.

"Rory!" I yell over the lump in my throat. "What if they're hurt?"

"You know I can't stop, miss," he apologizes with his eyes fixed on the road before him. "I'm sure they're fi—"

Rory's words are cut short when a pickup truck darts from an alleyway and slams into the driver's side of our SUV, causing my body to bounce around the backseat like a ragdoll. My head bangs against the window, and my vision goes hazy and begins to blacken around the edges.

"Quinn... Quinn!" Rory's shouting of my name grows increasingly louder as he pulls at me from the front. "Come on, Quinn. Fucking wake up."

Pushing myself from the seat, I grumble at the pain radiating through my scalp. I apply pressure in an attempt to alleviate the throbbing, only to wince when my palm presses against my wet, sticky hair.

"My leg is pinned," Rory tries to hide his panic. "They're coming for us. You need to go."

My heart thumps painfully as panic races through me, only amplifying the pounding in my head. Shaking my head, I mutter, "No. I... I can't."

"Get out of the car, Quinn," he orders. "I'll slow them for as long as I can."

"Rory..." I plead, both terrified to stay in the car and be outside of it with no one to protect me.

"Run," he demands. "Run, and don't fucking stop for anyone."

Kicking off my heels, I push open the door and slide from the backseat. I run from the SUV and toward the nearest side street. The asphalt tears at the bottom of my feet, and the impact of every stride shoots through my skull.

A gunshot fires behind me. Then another. The loud pops reverberate off the surrounding buildings. There are so many deafening shots that I can't tell which are real and which are echoes. They fire in the distance for what seems like minutes before coming to an abrupt stop, the silence alerting me to the shoes pounding against the pavement behind me.

I turn just in time to see a large man lunging at me. His arms wrap around me, and I scream as he violently pulls me from the ground.

CHAPTER FORTY-ONE
DECLAN

Conor, Finn, and Rory were leaving the house with Quinn no more than a few minutes after us. They should've been here at least twenty fucking minutes ago.

Father O'Flaherty places his hand on my shoulder and gives it a gentle squeeze. "Are you sure she's coming, son?"

Of course she's fucking coming.

"Yes," I insist. "My brothers are bringing her."

The idea of Quinn having cold feet is so outlandish that it's laughable. She's wanted this for most of her life. There aren't words to describe how excited she is—*we are*—about this day finally being here. It could be nothing more than an accident on the FDR, but my gut is telling me otherwise.

Something is wrong.

Stepping from the altar, I pull my phone from my pocket and call Finn. It rings a few times and goes to voicemail. When I call Conor, I'm met with the same unnerving result.

Something is definitely wrong.

"Try calling Finn again," I huff at Liam as I pace anxiously between the flower adorned pews. "I'm going to try Rory."

"Voicemail," Liam informs me, moments before Rory's phone diverts to voicemail as well.

"Well, keep fucking trying," I snarl, hitting the button to dial Rory again. Every repeated dial is met with the same results.

"Come here, *a stóirín*." I pull her from the pew before the altar, her adorable, fluffy dress crinkling as I lift her into my arms. "*Daidi* needs to go."

"Go?" She looks confused as I hastily carry her toward Layla and Tristan. "I want to see Quinn in her princess dress, *daidi*."

Me too, a stóirín.

"I need you to take her home." I hug Fiona tightly and pass her into Tristan's arms. "Something isn't right, Tris."

"Go." He nods. "Take Liam with you. Don't worry about Fiona. You know Layla and I will take care of her."

Cupping the back of her head, I pull her toward me and tenderly kiss her forehead. "I love you, *a stóirín*."

As I storm out of the church, Liam is immediately on my heel. We stop at the back of the SUV and open the liftgate to arm ourselves from the concealed unit beneath the cargo area. With a pistol stowed in my waistband and a short-barreled shotgun in hand, I climb into the driver's seat and wait for Liam to join me.

"If you make a left and go down four or five blocks, it'll put you right on the FDR," Liam directs as I wait for a break in traffic to pull into the street. We both know the route they were supposed to be taking. It makes the most sense to retrace their steps as we head toward the house.

We barely make it two blocks from the church before finding ourselves in gridlock. Barely moving, we creep down the block. "For fuck's sake," I blare on the horn. "Get the fuck out the way."

I catch a glimpse of a police cruiser parked in the middle of the road. The lights are flashing, and the officer standing before it is detouring traffic down a side street to get around an accident. Following the cars before me, I'm slam on the brakes when I see it.

"What the fuck?" Liam jerks forward from the sudden stop.

"That's our fucking car!" I leave the engine running as I jump from the driver's seat, not caring that the SUV is in the middle of the road. Pushing past the police barricade, I race toward Quinn. Every stride grants me a clearer view of the scene before me. And the sight before me causes my feet to grow heavier, like I'm wading through tar.

No less than eight Bratva soldiers lie on the road between me and the SUV, all of them lifeless in growing pools of blood. Bullet casings and shotgun shells float in the claret surrounding them and roll across the asphalt. Even with the strong breeze, the smell of gunpowder lingers in the air.

Firefighters and paramedics work diligently to pull Rory from the driver's seat. His dress shirt is a deep crimson, and his suit glistens from the amount of blood that has saturated it. As he clings to life, our eyes meet, and the sense of failure in his nearly breaks me. I don't need to reach the him to know what he needs to tell me. *She's gone.* Rory mouths, "I'm sorry, Sir."

He's being pulled from the bullet-ridden car and placed on a stretcher when I finally really reach him. I clutch his hand, and he uses what little strength he has to pull toward him. Struggling to breathe, losing blood with every shallow breath, he gurgles, "I tried to save her. I tried. I'm sor—"

"Rory!" I shout his name as his hand falls limp in mine.

Someone grabs me from behind, pulling me away from Rory as they rush him toward an awaiting ambulance, "You can't be here, sir."

"That's my fucking car," I shout, staring at the splintered

rear window covered in blood. *Her blood.* "And my fucking wife."

"Your wife?" The officer continues to pull me away from the scene.

Conor and Finn both stagger toward me as the officer pulls me further from the vehicle. Blood oozes from a large gash in Conor's forehead, and he's holding his left arm as it hangs lower than it should, clearly pulled out of the socket. Finn isn't in much better shape, with blood trickling from the bruised and blooded cut above his eye. A paramedic follows them, arguing to let her help them as they walk faster to get to me.

"Get off my fucking brother," Conor's voice booms at the man holding me. Using his good arm, he tears him off me and tosses him to the ground as if he weighs nothing. Neither of us can get to the SUV fast enough.

I pull at the handle, unable to open the thoroughly dented door. Finn slams his fist through the cracked glass, and I almost can't look as it shatters into the backseat and rains down the door to the pavement. Bloody streaks run along the door beneath the open window, and crimson stains the tan leather.

But she's not here.

All that's left of her are a pair of white high heels marbled with her bloody fingerprints.

I'm so sorry, mo chéadsearc.

I broke my promise...again.

CHAPTER FORTY-TWO
QUINN

"Uhhhhhhh," I groan. Pain radiates through every inch of my body as I stir. I can't help but think how much the cold metal beneath me—although uncomfortable—provides a little bit of relief.

Cold metal?

Struggling through the stabbing pain in my head, I force myself to open my eyes, only managing to flutter my eyelids when I'm met with the blindingly bright lights. I try desperately to make myself adjust to the oppressive shine as I try to sift through the hazy recollection of what happened.

The accident...

Gunshots.

So many gunshots.

Oh my God, Rory!

My heart throbs, suddenly thinking the worst. He might not have ever said much, but the man has been watching over me for months.

Running.

The stench of cigarettes as my feet were yanked from the ground.

The odor from my memory is so vivid that I can feel the burn in my nostrils and the faint taste of the burned tobacco on my tongue. Both turn my stomach.

Clutching at my throat and gasping for air, my vision slowly goes black around the edges as a harrowing voice whispers in my ear, "Go to sleep, honey. I don't want to have to hurt you... yet."

I involuntarily suck in a deep inhale, as though my body needs to ensure I'm still breathing. My nostrils suddenly fill with the same distinctive scent as though I am completely surrounded by it. The warm stench wafts over my face, and I gag as it singes my lungs when I accidentally suck it in. Hacking the vile air from my lungs, I force my eyes open.

It's him!

The man from the alley is a cigarette's length from my face, occupying the entirety of my vision. With his eyes fully fixated on mine, he sucks in a slow, deep drag as I try to scurry away from him, only to find my back against the cold, metal wall. The sudden dread of being boxed in causes me to panic, only worsening my ability to draw in a proper breath. Smoke billows from his nostrils as he leans closer and exhales. "Welcome back, honey. We've all been waiting for you to wake up."

My eyes dart from his dark gaze upon hearing the word 'all,' confirming exactly what I was dreading. The cold metal I'm pressed firmly against is the inside of a van. The windows on the rear doors are covered with newspaper, and from my vantage point, I can't see over the dash. The way the metal vibrates beneath me, I know we're going fast.

Far from Declan...

...from all the boys and Fiona..

There are two men sitting in the front bucket seats and another two sitting across from me by the rancid chimney. They're staring at me—*a look I know all too well*—and it has me dashing my gaze between them all. Pulling my legs into my chest, I wrap my arms around them tightly, trying desperately to comfort and protect myself.

"Are you shy, baby?" a man with a large scar running the length of his face asks. Closing the distance between us, he slides his hand up my leg. His touch causes bile to rise in my throat, and I struggle to keep it at bay as he continues to talk. "I didn't think you would be. You sure as fuck didn't look shy every time I've watched you."

The dark laughter of all the men fills the van, each hearty laugh and cackle chilling me to the bone.

"You're not shy, are you, honey?" the chimney chimes in, his eyes raking over my tightly curled body. "You love getting fucked like a little whore. You're going to love *everything* we have planned for you."

"Fuck you," I spit, almost regretting them as they echo painfully in my ears.

"Don't you worry your pretty little red head. I plan to *fuck you* plenty." He firmly grips my jaw, forcing my mouth open. The putrid taste of stale ash fills my mouth when he violently shoves his tongue past my lips. I shove at him, but he only laughs—forcing the stale air from his lungs into my mouth.

He tastes so vile that I actually enjoy the metallic taste of copper when his blood hits my tongue. Fighting against the pain of his tight hold, I continue to bite down hard and force my teeth through the thick muscle of his tongue. I don't stop until his warm blood spills over my lips and runs down my chin.

"You fucking whore," he shouts the nearly unrecognizable words around his swollen—and, unfortunately, still attached—tongue as the back of his hand strikes my face. It radiates around my already throbbing skull so painfully that I have to fight against my fading vision. With blood pouring down his chin, he raises his hand to strike me again.

"Enough!" a deep Russian-accented voice shouts from the passenger seat, and the chimney immediately lowers his hand and retreats to his side of the van. "Pretty sure you were told not to lay fucking hand on her. Maybe next time you'll fucking listen."

"Thank you," I whisper, using the tulle of my dress to wipe the blood from my chin.

"Don't thank me, sweetheart," the man from the passenger seat turns and tosses a handkerchief into my lap. "I'm just delivering you to the boss as he asked."

CHAPTER FORTY-THREE
DECLAN

I drive my fist through the liftgate window of the Suburban and don't so much as flinch when the glass tears through my flesh. My fists drive dents into the metal as I curse God.

Benevolent my ass.

There is nothing benevolent about wrenching those I love from me. Forcing me to watch Sarah endure grueling rounds of chemo for a year, only to watch her die a slow and painful death, wasn't kind. There is nothing compassionate about letting the Bratva steal Quinn from me—on our wedding day, no less. I can only imagine what they plan to do to her; it cannot even remotely be described as humane.

Blood trickles over my fingers as I continue to split the skin of my knuckles, pounding my anger and guilt into the vehicle before me.

"Dec." Conor rests his hand on my shoulder, trying to reel me back in. I shove him away from me and am ready to throw my next punch into his face. He takes a step back and lifts his good hand into the air in a truce. "You need to stop, Dec."

I slam my fist into the dented metal once more and find myself ensnared in a tight embrace. Gripping his own wrists in front of my chest, Liam tightens his hold. "For fuck's sake!" he snarls. "Breaking your fucking hands isn't going to do a fucking thing to bring her back home."

"Let go of me, you fucking prick," I shout, trying to free myself from his hold. "Liam, let the fuck go of me."

"Yell at me," Liam demands.

Continuing to fight against his encircled arms, I cause us both to topple backward to the hard pavement. We land on our asses with a thud, but Liam maintains the firm hold he has around me. "I swear to Christ, I'll fucking kill you if you don't let go of me."

"That's it. Fucking yell. Shout at me," Liam insists as he wrestles his legs around me to subdue me. "Yell at us. Be fucking mad. Get it all fucking out!"

I wrestle against him, my rage-fueled roars laced with fear and grief-filled sobs slowly fading. He holds me until the violent screams subside. "I won't fucking lose her. I can't," I growl, shaking my head.

I already lost her once. I can't grieve her again. It will break me.

Liam releases his grip on me and lets his arms fall from my chest as Finn stretches his hand out. "Now, get your arse off the ground, old man, so we can go bring your wife fucking home." Blinking back angry tears, I slap my hand into his, and he helps me from the pavement.

Turning, I forward the favor to Liam. I grip the back of his neck and pull him into me when he reaches his feet. He hugs me back as I thank him.

"*Rud ar bith do mo dheartháir*," Liam shares the motto that has kept us strong our whole lives. *For my brother.* All of us are extensions of each other, willing to do or sacrifice anything for them that we would do for ourselves. "Let's go find this asshole and rescue Quinn."

The four of us push through the growing crowd around the accident to my SUV, still sitting in the middle of the intersection. We ignore the police officer shouting at us as we approach it. Liam takes the driver's seat, and I climb into the back with Conor. "You're going to need to get this looked at," I feel his shoulder, confirming that it is, in fact, dislocated.

"The fuck I am," he huffs. "This isn't shit. Just pop it back in."

"You can't be serious." Liam cranes his head between the front seats.

"Just fucking do it," Conor confirms.

Turning in my seat, I lift his arm and wedge my foot under his armpit. "On three. This is going to hu—"

I yank hard, the pop of the joint realigning—and Conor roaring in pain—fills the tight confines. "Mother fucking, cocksucker!" he exclaims. "I'd rather be fucking shot next time."

"Don't be a little bitch," Finn huffs from the front seat.

"A little bitch?" Conor swiftly reaches around the seat and slaps Finn in the forehead. His palm lands right on the cut above his eye, and he winces in pain. "I'll show you a little bitch."

My phone buzzes, and I pull it from my pocket, expecting it to be a text from Tristan, confirming that he has arrived home safely with *a stóirín*. Instead, it's a text message from an unknown number. When I swipe it open, I don't need a name to know who it's from.

UNKNOWN

Don't worry, Declan.

I'll send you plenty of pictures so you know exactly what you're missing.

Enraged, I kick the back of Liam's seat. "FUCK!" Expelling my anger as another message pops up, and I see my bride for the first time.

She would've been fucking gorgeous walking down the aisle.

Dried blood mats her disheveled hair to her forehead and side of her face. Her face has been wiped clean, but the trails of blood running under her chin and to the delicate lace of her dress are impossible to miss. While it's obvious she's afraid, I know that look in her eyes. She's fucking mad.

Stay mad, mo chéadsearc.

Fucking fight them with everything you've got.

I'm coming.

I won't fail you again.

Another message comes through, and I fight back a villainous chuckle.

> For her sake, I hope she learns how to behave.

Not fucking likely.

CHAPTER FORTY-FOUR
QUINN

The front of the chimney's shirt is stained scarlet from the bloody waterfall created by the deep wound I left on his tongue. It has slowed substantially, but bloody spittle continues to trickle down his chin.

And he's fucking pissed.

Declan would be proud as hell of me.

I'm fucking proud of me.

His eyes haven't left me since his hand crashed against my face, and the ire only seems to grow with each passing minute. Even though I'm quite certain I'm going to pay dearly for nearly severing half of his tongue, I know beyond a doubt that it was fucking worth it.

If nothing else, he'll think twice about putting that vile tongue—or anything else—near my mouth again.

While I might be absolutely terrified about what I can only imagine they're going to do to me, I'm not going to close my eyes and lay there while it happens. For months, all I could think about was how weak I was for not being able to fight off the men who attacked me in the bar. The self-imposed guilt was crippling.

I might be scared—*fucking **terrified***—but I'm not weak. Nothing about me is weak. Running my finger over the scar, I can almost hear Declan in my ear. *It's a reminder of how fucking strong you are. Of how determined you are to live.* I repeat them to myself over and over again.

I just got the life I've always wanted, and I'm not ready to give it up yet. Fuck, do I ever want to live!

We finally pull to a stop, with the gruff man sitting up front exiting first and pulling open the double doors at the back of the van. "Out," he commands, looking at me.

Pain radiates through me when I move, causing me to hesitate. Quickly irritated with me, he snarls, "Get the fuck out of the van, or I will pull you out by the fucking hair."

Crawling on my all-fours like an animal, my knees dig into the metal as I gingerly make my way to him. He grips my bicep painfully hard, tearing me from the van. I struggle to find my footing, and the balls of my feet drags across the asphalt. I wince in pain as it adds more scrapes to the already tender flesh.

"Move," he yanks, dragging me toward a six-story Art Deco building. He pulls me along the sidewalk. I nearly scream for help when I see people walking toward us, stopping when I notice them all avert their eyes when they see me.

I'm yanked by the arm until we reach an apartment on the top floor. The gruff Russian shoves me into a forest-green, upholstered chair, and I rub at my arm where he held a vise grip on me. "Stay," he demands.

Not that there's anywhere to go.

This building has as much security as Declan's apartment. The only difference is that these men are easy to spot—their weapons on clear display for people to know who they are and threatening them to keep their distance.

The gruff Russian returns with a tall, shirtless man. Tattoos cover every inch of his exposed skin. My eyes are drawn to the thieves' stars covering both of his shoulders, marking him as a high-ranking member of the Bratva. His eyes roam over me as he crosses the room between us. "I hear you've already been a handful," he grumbles, planting his hands on the arms of the chair.

I lean back in the chair as he continues to press forward, "Am I going to need to restrain you... What is it he calls you... Mo Head Shark?"

"Mo chéadsearc," I harshly correct his atrocious pronunciation. "And what do I call you? Cocksucker? Or Motherfucker?"

"You can call me Emil." He laughs, and I'm surprised by the glimmer in his dark eyes and the tug of a smile at the corner of his mouth. "You are a feisty fucking bitch, aren't you?" He drags a knuckle along my jaw, and I flinch at his touch.

"Up," he orders. I ignore his command and stay firmly seated in the chair. His hand wraps around my throat, and he squeezes tightly before using it as leverage to make me stand. "I fucking said 'up.'"

He maintains his firm grasp even after he's gotten me to my feet. I struggle to breathe through the tight hold. Tipping his head to the side, he squeezes harder, and his eyes grow wide as he watches me. My heart begins to pound, and my lungs burn as he starves me of oxygen. Desperately needing to breathe, I claw at his hand and try futilely to free myself from his fingers.

"You might find it benefits you to fucking listen when I tell you to do something." His voice is deep and gravelly. "I'm going to have very little patience for that smart fucking mouth of yours."

I gasp violently for air when he releases me, choking on it when it finally fills my lungs.

"Come." Emil grips my wrist and pulls me through his apartment. Reaching a bedroom, I pause. When I see the bed a few yards from me, my feet suddenly have the weight of cement blocks.

I am fucking strong, and I want to fucking live.

He roughly yanks me through the open doorway. "I also have little patience for your inability to listen."

Relief washes over me as he drags me past the bed and into the attached bathroom. It's a fleeting feeling, immediately wisked away when he turns on the shower and demands, "Strip. And do not make me ask you twice."

With trembling hands, I grip the loose ends of the bow at my back and undo it. The bodice of my dress becomes lax, and Emil crosses his arms as he waits. Slipping the spaghetti straps from my shoulder, my blood-soaked, ruined wedding dress slides down my body and into a fluffy cloud around my feet. Standing in nothing but my panties, I cover my breasts with my arms.

"Panties, too." Emil's eyes dart to my white lacy thong. Taking a deep breath, I push the material over my hips and let it fall down my legs. A deep grumble rattles from him, and the hairs on the back of my neck stand on end when he groans, "A *natural* redhead."

I am strong. I want to fucking live.

"You can relax." His tone is sincere. "As much as I want to see if that little pussy of yours is as enjoyable to use as it is to watch, I won't be taking my turn with you quite yet. The Pakhan wants you passed through the ranks to teach both you and those fucking Evans brothers a lesson. He has demanded he gets to be the first to fuck you, and luckily for you, he won't be back from Mother Russia until tomorrow."

His confession is as comforting as it is terrifying.

"Shower," he demands, pulling back the curtain and signaling for me to enter. "I might not be able to put my cock in you, but I have other ways of making you listen."

CHAPTER FORTY-FIVE

DECLAN

Finn walks into the kitchen as he shoves his phone back into his pocket. "I just got off the phone with that hot nurse that works New York General—"

"The psycho one who tried to stab you?" Liam interrupts him.

"She wasn't psycho. She was just really fucking mad that I fucked her best friend," Finn corrects him, and I try unsuccessfully to hold back my sigh of annoyance.

"Finnigan!" I huff. "What the fuck does this have to do with Quinn."

"Nothing," he responds, and I nearly climb over the counter to kick his arse. "Rory. I called her about Rory."

"And?" Conor asks the question we are all wondering the answer to.

"He's still in surgery, but it looks promising," he shares, and we all collectively expel a sigh of relief.

Rory might not be blood like the men in this room, but after today, he is no less an Evans than any of them. He might not have been successful, but he was more than willing to give his life to protect Quinn.

He didn't fail her. I did.

I never should have given in to her insistence for a stupid tradition.

We've all been back home for hours and have made no progress toward figuring out where she was taken . These fucking Bratva, for as brazen as they are, they hide like fucking cockroaches when the lights turn on. In the hours that we've been back here, we haven't made it any further.

Me foolishly expecting different does not differ from expecting a miracle.

"Between the lot of us, we must know someone. Anyone that can give us a shred of useful information." I flex my hands and groan at the soreness of my cracked and bruising knuckles. "We have to do something. I can't fucking lose her."

I promised I would protect her and that I would keep her safe. We might not have sworn it before God yet, but I promised her a life with me.

"We are trying, Dec," Tristan imparts. "Every last one of us is doing everything we can."

"It's not fucking enough," I roar as my aching hands

pound against the countertop. It won't be enough until we bring her back home.

Hours pass—*too many hours*—and I'm ready to start making my way through Brighton Beach door by door until I uncover something that will help me find her.

Liam's phone buzzes on the counter, and he looks at it. His expression gives me the faintest bit of hope. "It's Kira," he announces.

After I killed Akim, Liam did exactly what he had said he would. Or he tried. He offered to get Kira out of the city and far away from servicing men like Akim had planned for her when he held her hostage. She made it no further than Westchester County before turning and running back into the brutal arms of the Bratva. Apparently, the abusive life she'd been living was less terrifying than the unknown.

The last time he checked on her, she had latched onto a mid-level soldier. A now ugly fuck who took one hell of a beating, leaving a scar running along his face to win the privilege of securing her as his personal whore.

Liam answers the phone on speaker, and her timid voice cracks through the phone, "I shouldn't be talking to you. Yuri will kill me just for knowing that I called."

"I... We can protect you from Yuri," Liam promises.

"I overheard him," she sobs quietly into the phone, "He was so mad about some redhead. He kept rambling that she was going to ruin his plan."

"His plan?"

"He was going to offer me to the Pakhan. Send me back to Russia so the Pakhan would give him more power." Her voice is soft, but she rambles her terrified thoughts, "I can't go back. Not... Not with him. Akim let him... Once... He's an evil fucking man, and I can't be his. I know the redhead is yours."

"How do you know?" I blurt, unable to control myself.

"Yuri kept rambling about how the Evans were going to fuck up everything for him. Because Emil had gotten his hands on the girl who killed the Pakhan's lieutenant. The Evans gir— Shit, Yuri is coming."

"Kira?" I call her name when the line goes silent, a muffled conversation the only indicator that Kira is still on the other end of the phone. We listen to the muffled yelling on the other end for minutes.

"I'm not calling for her. I'm calling for me," Kira admits through sobs when she comes back on the line. "I'll tell you where to find her if you promise to take me, too."

"Yes," I agree without glancing at my brothers or even remotely thinking it through.

"I need you to promise."

"I swear on my life," I vow. "I will do anything for you if it means you will help get my wife back to me."

"I will text you the address," she whispers before the line goes dead.

I'm coming for you mo chéadsearc.

Tristan paces for a moment. Always the pragmatic one, he huffs, "This could be a trap."

"It could be." I nod in agreement.

"They could be using Kira to get to us," Conor concurs.

"They could be. It could also be the only chance I have to get Quinn back. The only chance before they force her on a plane and she disappears forever… To a life she'll never survive."

I don't know if I could survive with the guilt of knowing what she would be enduring. Shaking my head, I sigh. "I'll go alone if I have to."

"Fuck that!" Finn shouts. "If you think I'm going to let you go alone after those assholes ruined my face, you've got another thing coming."

Conor smirks. "And I'm fucking pissed they totaled my Escalade."

"I'm not going to let you fucks go kill a bunch of Bratva assholes without me," Liam states matter-of-factly.

All of us look to Tristan. "You know how I feel." He shakes his head. "*Rud ar bith do mo dheartháir.*"

CHAPTER FORTY-SIX
QUINN

The soft glow of the early morning light basks through the window as I rub my hand over my swollen belly. The soft, rhythmic flutter against my hand is a beautiful reminder of our baby growing inside of me.

Climbing from bed and standing in the window, I stare over the Long Island Sound behind the home that Declan and I are rapidly filling with children. The shouting, laughter, and children running are all nearly constant. It's loud, but it's beautiful. A home bursting at the seams with love, just as Declan had promised me.

The loudest of the bunch are the twins, two rambunctious little boys who stare up at me with the same beautiful oceanic eyes as their father. Fiona, who is growing so fast, looks more and more like her beautiful late mother every day. And this little girl in my belly, I can't wait to see if she bears her father's dark hair or my red locks, as we add a little sister to our ever-growing home.

I dreamed of the life I wanted with Declan for years. But the life he has given me is beyond anything I had ever imagined.

Waking, I splay my hand over my belly, unable to shake how real my dream felt. With my palm pressed against my flat stomach, the flutter of a kicking baby beneath it tickles my pain, and I sigh contently for a moment. The beautiful flutter of *our* baby.

I don't know if it's real or if it's just a dream, but the thought of a little girl growing inside of me is one more reason to be strong.

I will be going home.

...To my family.

"Sweet dreams, *mo chéadsearc?*" Emil smirks as he watches me sleep on the couch.

"Please don't call me that," I snip. He's not allowed to fuck me—*rape me*—and I think he's equally as hesitant to leave a mark on me. The worst he has done to me is wrap his hands around my throat and watch me shower and dress. "I am not your first love. I am not your love. I am nothing more than a hole you're waiting for your boss to give you permission to put your cock in."

"You're more than one hole," he snidely replies as he walks toward me and hovers over where I sit. "You're three holes and a remarkable pair of tits. All of which I look forward to putting cock in and covering in cum. Unless, of course, the Pakhan decides to keep you... Or you aren't strong enough for what he's going to want."

Strong enough?

He's baiting me. I know it. Yet I can't stop myself from wanting to know more, even though I know the answer will only add to the terrifying images I'm already trying to keep at bay. I look up at him and ask, "What he's going to want?"

"The Pakhan maintains a harem of women for a reason," Emil shares. "He enjoys inflicting pain on his *whores*. Those who find his sadistic needs tolerable—or survivable—become a challenge, and he needs to break them." Emil reaches down and gathers my hair into his hand as I try to recoil from his touch. Fisting it hard, he yanks my head backward so roughly that I cry out in pain as the burn radiates at my crown. "If he decides he wants you, you'll spend the rest of your life wishing that you'd *only* have to bear the wrath of me and my men."

Nothing makes you question your mental health quite like the moment a non-consensual gang bang seems more appealing than being gifted to the sadistic owner of a harem.

He releases my hair and pulls me from the couch by my wrist. "You need to get ready. He'll be arriving shortly, and as much as I would prefer to keep you and watch your cunt squirt at my hand, I'm going to be a good soldier and prepare you for him."

Shoving me into the bathroom, he turns on the shower and holds a razor before me. "Can you trim your cunt yourself, or do you need a little help?" I snatch the razor from his hand, not wanting him anywhere near between my thighs, as he snickers.

Fuck, men can be appalling.

"Your cunt is perfect as is," he croons as he eyes my pussy. "Use it for your legs."

After showering, Emil has me put on a much too-tight and too-short black dress, topping it off with a pair of too-tall stilettos. Having all my weight on the balls of my feet, currently covered with abrasions from running barefoot, makes the shoes practically unbearable.

Walking past a mirror, I am caught off guard by my reflection. The mini dress is a far cry from the way I walked out of my home yesterday afternoon.

And my face...

While I'm trying desperately to keep my fear buried deep, it's still the first thing I see when I look into my eyes. No matter how hard I try, I cannot force the smile I had, knowing I was on my way to the church to marry Declan.

We were so close...

A heavy knock at the door startles me, tearing me back to the present.

Emil's gaze meets mine in my reflection, and he firmly instructs, "I expect you to behave yourself."

CHAPTER FORTY-SEVEN
DECLAN

From the moment Kira's call ended, I have been pacing the patio that runs along the length of our home as we wait. The hours that pass feel like days as we all wait for Kira to send a follow-up text of where she—*and Quinn*—will be tonight. My brothers take turns coming out to give me updates, most of which are insignificant, giving them the opportunity to check on me. They know me —*maybe better than I know myself*—and can see that I am holding it together by a thread.

A thread that I can't allow to break.

The sun is sinking over the horizon, and the last of the amber light dances on the surface of the water as darkness begins to cloak everything. The wait for this information has been so long that I'm beginning to think it isn't coming. If Yuri catches on to Kira's plan, he could prevent her from reaching out to us, or worse. It doesn't matter which; losing Kira in any capacity will completely sever the only lifeline I have to getting Quinn back.

My brothers have been a little more productive while we wait. Both the Suburban and the Tahoe in the driveway are loaded with enough weapons and ammunition that they could be considered an armory; at some point, Finn mentioned needing to grab an anti-tank missile from his apartment. *Something we should all probably address with him later.* They've ensured I'm well-armed, too, with two Sig Sauer pistols tucked into a holster at the rear of my pants. Not knowing what we're walking into, I also have a KA-BAR knife hooked to my belt and four additional magazines secured at the front of the holster. I can only assume my brothers are equally as strapped with weapons, leaving us collectively prepared to attack a small country.

Dec!" Liam shouts, knocking on the wall of glass separating us to get my attention. When I turn toward him, he presses the lit-up phone to the glass. "She sent it."

Heading inside, I find Conor, Liam, and Finn heading out the front door as Tristan takes a moment to say goodbye to Layla. I give him a moment—*the moment I would want with Quinn*—before approaching to say goodbye to Fiona, who's sitting beside her.

"I love you, *mo chuisle*." Tristan places a final kiss on Layla's lips before turning his attention to me. "I'll be outside."

After taking a few moments to compose myself, I lift Fiona from the couch and pull her into my arms, holding her tightly and inhaling deeply. "*Daidi* has to leave for a little bit."

"Can I come?" she asks with a broad smile.

"Not this time, *a stóirín*. I need you to be a big girl for me. Make sure you listen to Layla, okay?" She nods her response. I stare at her for a moment, deploring this situation and the impossible choice the Bratva are forcing me to make. "*Daidi* loves you so very much, *a stóirín*."

"I love you too, *daidi*." She wraps her little arms around my neck as she places a sticky kiss on my cheek. Pulling in, I hold her tightly to me. If this is the last hug I ever give her, I want her to remember it. "*Daidi*, you're squishing me."

"It's just because I love you too much." I release her from my embrace and place a kiss on her forehead before lowering her bare little feet to the floor.

"Take care of her," I plead as I pull Layla in for a hug.

She nods against my chest, knowing exactly what it is I am truly asking of her. "Like she were my own, Declan."

Her words are all I need to hear, and I turn on my heel and head straight toward my brothers and climb into the passenger seat of the Suburban with Tristan and Finnigan. Liam and Conor are going to follow immediately behind us in the Tahoe, ensuring we have two options to get the fuck out of Brighton Beach with Quinn when this is over.

I glance at the GPS as we pull through the gates. We won't be arriving at the address Kira gave us for nearly ninety minutes.

A fucking eternity.

With the five of us communicating via Bluetooth in the cars, Liam works on his laptop to learn all he can about where we are going. It's a historic apartment building, which comes with advantages and disadvantages compared to storming someone's home. A bigger building like this makes it easier for us to slip inside unnoticed. Unfortunately, it also means there are a lot more people inside—innocents and Bratva.

The odds are not in our favor here. They took Quinn. The manpower Emil had to make that happen, I can only imagine he is a lieutenant—or at least in line to become one after what he has already accomplished.

And, the Pakhan is coming.

"This is a fucking suicide mission," I grumble as we discuss the amount of firepower the Bratva is going to have in and around this building. "We'll never even get through the front fucking door."

Liam's voice billows through the speakers, "What if… What if we don't go through the front door."

"Oh, fuck yes!" Finn exclaims. "Let me a blow a fucking hole in the side of that bitch!"

"Not what I meant, Finnigan." I can practically see Liam shaking his head as he responds to Finn.

CHAPTER FORTY-EIGHT
QUINN

When Emil opens the door to his apartment, I am surprised at the face on the other side. *The scar.* I can't imagine *he* is the Pakhan. At least, not after what happened in the van. That would be like any of the Evans boys sitting by idly as one of their men outright disobeyed an order in front of them.

No...

He's someone else.

"Yuri," Emil greets him, his demeanor turning cold. "I didn't realize you were bringing a guest."

"Kira," he discloses, leading her over the threshold and into the room. The look in her light-blue eyes is undeniable. She's scared. *Terrified.* I know because it's the same look I saw in my own when I stared at my reflection just moments ago. "She's a gift."

"A gift?" Emil scoffs at the notion, and as I am looking at her I don't understand his reaction. The young—maybe twenty-something—blonde standing in front of me is absolutely beautiful. She's tall and lean with minimal curves. Her face mimics her body—slender, perfectly proportionate, and with cheekbones that most women would kill to have without contouring. If it weren't for the bruises on her arms and neck, she looks like she could own the catwalk at any fashion show. "Kira is not a gift for the Pakhan. She's my late father's whore. Grand Central Station has seen less men than her cunt."

"Maybe," Yuri admits, "But it still makes for an enjoyable fuck. Give her a try if you don't believe me."

Emil looks at me, his eyes hungrily roam over my exposed skin in this tiny dress, before responding, "I tend not to put my dick in holes that have been fucked by my father."

That couldn't be further from the truth.

He'd happily fuck her if he weren't hoping for the opportunity to be putting his cock in me tonight.

"Your loss." Yuri shrugs. Swiping Kira's long blonde hair over her shoulder, he further exposes the massive marbled purple and green bruise running along her neck and down her shoulder. "I've been training her for him. She fucking loves pain. He'll be able to do so much with her before she becomes useless to him. She is very much *a gift.*"

My stomach churns as I continue to listen to these men talk about her. To them, she barely even constitutes property. She's nothing more than a set of tight holes to them. Something for them to fuck, torture, and dispose of when she no longer meets their needs. I'm not naïve. I know that men like this exist in the world, but seeing it —*hearing it*—might be the most disturbing thing I have been through.

And that's saying a lot.

As they continue to talk, it's not lost on me that they view me the same way. Emil will *gift me* to the Pakhan to endure what I would likely only wish was a short life. Or he'll keep me until he tires of me and begins offering me to his colleagues like Yuri.

"Have you tried the Evans' whore?" Yuri inquires a little too eagerly.

"Not yet." His dark eyes wander toward me. "I didn't want her tasting like condoms or dripping with my cum if he decided he wanted to sample her."

Sample me? Am I fucking appetizer platter?

I swallow back vomit when the taste of bile hits the back of my tongue, barely managing to keep it down as Emil ushers me and Kira to the couch. The men—*a recognition they don't deserve*—leave us for a moment in the living room as they disappear to the kitchen in search of drinks.

"Your husband is coming," Kira whispers so quietly that I think I'm imagining the barely audible words.

Needing to know if she said what I think—*and unsure if she means the man I want to marry or the one I might be forced to*—I try to remain quiet when I whisper, "What?"

She waits for Yuri to turn his back. "Your husband and his brothers... The Evans... They are coming."

"You know Declan?" I excitedly whisper louder than intended and am relieved when I find that my outburst doesn't draw the attention of Yuri or Emil.

"Declan? No. Liam. He tried to save me." She lightly shakes her head, "I should have let him."

A knock brings Yuri and Emil back to the living room, immediately silencing our conversation and removing any ability I have to ask the thousands of questions racing through my thoughts. Emil opens the door and greets the Pakhan reverently before drawing his attention to me and Kira.

The Pakhan is younger than I expected, roughly the same age as Declan. He's a massive man, making even Conor seem small. Tattoos cover so much of his skin that his hands are practically black, and ink flares up his neck and onto parts of his face. His eyes meet mine and ice runs through my veins at their darkness. There is nothing behind them. They are soulless, just like I imagine them to be.

"She's prettier in person than I expected," he tells the other men and licks his lips hungrily as he continues to hold his dark gaze on me.

Please hurry, Declan.

Please hurry, Declan.

CHAPTER FORTY-NINE

DECLAN

Parking down the block from the address Kira provided, we climb from our respective SUVs and each grab a larger gun from the cargo areas in silence. The five of us are cloaked in black and armed to the hilt. We stand without speaking beside the Tahoe for a moment, every one of us praying that we all make it through what we are about to walk into.

Finn cocks his shotgun, breaking the silence. "Let's go get your fucking wife."

It's all that's needed to kick us into gear. We make our way to the building next to our destination, taking the alleyway to stay out of sight. Using his good shoulder, Conor barrels through the rear door of the building and holds it open to let us all inside.

"Such a gentleman," Finn quips.

He loves this shit a little too much.

I'm worried about saving Quinn and getting home safely to Fiona. Getting us all home safely. Meanwhile, he's probably fucking hard at the thought of filling Bratva soldiers with bullets.

Do yourself a favor, don't fucking ask!

Finding the stairwell, we make our way to the roof. Moving slowly and using the door for cover, in case there are Bratva on the opposing roof, Finn steps outside. Surveying the area, he whispers, "There are two men walking the length of the roof. They should have their backs turned to us in a minute, maybe two."

"Hold this." Finn shoves his shotgun at me and pulls a knife from his belt. Peering around Liam, he takes off running toward them.

"Fucking hell," Liam huffs, dropping his shotgun. Following Finn's action, Liam is immediately on his heel. Both of them running at full speed toward the ledge. When they reach it, they hurdle the roughly four-foot gap between the buildings. They both crash into the two very surprised Bratva men, who never even heard them coming. Blood spills onto the rooftop as Finn slices through one man's throat, and Liam plunges his knife into the axillary artery of the other. By the time Tristan, Conor and I jump to the rooftop, the Bratva are both dead.

So far, so good.

As though the universe wants to continue to scoff at me, we find the door leading to the stairwell locked. Conor searches both dead men, but neither has any keys on them. Cocking my shotgun, I lift the barrel and aim it at the door. "They're about to know we're fucking here, then."

My finger flexes against the trigger, the gun milliseconds away from firing when the door pops open. The man on the other side gasps something in Russian. Equally as surprised to see him as he is me, I hesitate for a second before cracking the barrel of the gun against the side of his head. It doesn't debilitate him, but it buys enough time for me to rush him.

I tackle him, not realizing how short the landing is behind him. We both painfully tumble down the flight of stairs, each of us struggling for the upper hand when we are on solid ground. Pinning him beneath me, I wrap my hands around his throat and squeeze. He struggles, his hands clawing and slapping at my arms trying to break free. I thrust the weight of my body onto my hands his windpipe crack under the weight. I climb from him as he grabs his throat, terror welling in his eyes when he realizes he's a dead man.

They're all fucking dead men.

I'll kill them all to get to her.

After stepping over him, I traverse the stairs two at a time to make my way to the fire door for the sixth floor. The stomp of my boots on the metal stairs echoes through the stairwell, the reverberation only growing louder when my brothers follow. Knowing this hallway will be full of soldiers, I don't pause. I barrel through the door as I draw both pistols from my back, firing at the first men I see.

The deafening sound of gunshots in the tight hall grows increasingly louder when my brothers file into the hall behind me, and Bratva mercenaries return fire. Man after man, they fall as we continue toward the apartment at the end of the hall. The apartment where Kira said they'd be.

White-hot pain slices through my side, and I wince as I continue to storm down the hallway. My shirt grows wet, and I can feel the warm trickle running along my stomach. I don't need to look down to know I've been shot, The burning in my shoulder from the repeated recoil of my gun only adds to it, but I don't fucking care.

I need to get to her.

Reaching the door to the apartment first, I slam my shoulder against it. I'm about to do it a second time when Conor roars from behind, "Fucking cocksucker!!"

I turn to find him firmly holding his palm over his gut, blood slowly beginning to ooze through his fingers. Noticing my concern, he grunts, "I'm fine."

Glancing up from his stomach, I find a sea of armed Bratva soldiers racing toward us.

We're too fucking close.

This doesn't end with us on the wrong side of the door.

Quickly swapping the near-empty magazines on both my Sigs, I raise both toward the army rushing us and squeeze the trigger until both clips are done.

CHAPTER FIFTY
QUINN

A loud bang in the hallway startles me. I don't place the sound until I hear it again... And again. *Gunshots.* Some sound right outside the door and others far away.

Declan!

Emil, Yuri, and the Pakhan are all immediately on edge. Each of them scrambling to find a weapon as the shots grow fewer yet louder.

"You knew he would come for me," I gloat when Emil glances at me.

I knew he would come for me.

That they would all come for me.

There's a large thud against the apartment door, but it doesn't open. I expect another and for it to fly off its hinges as a swarm of Evans come flowing through. Instead, there's nothing but more gunfire.

"Get Quinn!" I hear Conor's deep voice boom over the repeated pops moments before another loud thud hits the door. It splinters from the frame and flies into the apartment, with Declan following directly behind it.

"Dec!" I scream, trying to warn him as I watch the three Russians raise their guns to shoot, but I'm too late. They all fire off a shot, and I watch his body jerk as one of the rounds hits his chest, the others—*thankfully*—missing their mark.

Declan falls to the ground, and a blood-curdling scream rises from my lungs as I try to push myself from the couch to get to him.

I can't lose him.

Not now.

Not after everything we've been through.

Finn fires from the threshold of the doorway, and both Yuri and Emil fall to the ground not far from Declan. His third shot hits the Pakhan. It knocks him off-kilter, but he grips the cream countertop of the small kitchen island and pulls himself to his feet. His eyes widen as the rest of the Evans brothers pour into the room. Turning his back, he blindly fires a few rounds as he retreats down the hall toward the fire escape.

Screaming his name as I rush forward, I fall to my knees when I reach Declan. I cannot contain my uncontrollable sobbing with fat tears streaming down my face. Moving on autopilot, I try to roll him onto his back. Liam joins me, easily flipping him over, and I gasp in horror at the sight. He hasn't just been shot in the chest. He has two other bullet wounds—one in his side, and another in his shoulder, about two inches above the round placed by the Pakhan.

"Dec, baby…" I weep as I stroke his face. "Please, baby… I just got you…"

"Shhh, *mo chéadsearc*," he groans, placing his hand over mine. "You aren't getting rid of me that easily."

Relieved beyond measure that he is still alive, I throw myself onto him to squeeze him tightly, causing him to grunt in pain. "I'm sorr–"

"Don't you dare be sorry." He pulls me back onto him and squeezes far too tightly. Yet, even though his embrace is so tight it hurts, I only want him to hold me closer. "I'd take a dozen more if it meant I got to touch you again.".

"This is super fucking sweet and all," Conor grits, clearly in pain of his own, "but you two do know that there are more fucking Bratva on their way, right?"

"Do we get to push your fucking Life Alert button, old man?" Finn hovers over us both. "Or do you think you can get your old arse off the floor?"

Even riddled with bullet wounds and in obvious pain, Declan looks as though he could spring from the floor to beat the piss out of Finn, who's smirking like nothing just happened.

And suddenly, I'm beyond certain that he's going to be perfectly fine.

CHAPTER FIFTY-ONE
DECLAN

Two days later...

"Declan Cathal Evans!" Quinn exclaims. "Get your ass back in that bed."

After leaving Emil's apartment, I apparently lost consciousness as we were going down the stairs of the adjacent building to get back to the Tahoe and Suburban. My recollection is fuzzy, but between everyone who has come to repeatedly check on me, I've managed to put the pieces together.

Liam and Tristan carried me down the stairs and a half block to the SUVs. When I was unceremoniously loaded into the back, they drove me to the nearest twenty-four-hour animal hospital, where some poor veterinarian was threatened at gunpoint to perform surgery on me. Losing blood faster than he could work, Liam, Tristan, and Finn all literally pumped their life into me to keep me alive.

Rud ar bith do mo dhearthair.

I continue to get out of the bed, pained. "If you're going to bark orders at me like that, *mo chéadsearc*, you better plan to be climbing into it as well, fully prepared to ride my cock. If not, I'm not staying in this fucking bed."

She throws her hands in the air, very aware that she is not going to win this argument with me. "At least let me get someone to help you downstairs."

"I can do it myself." I wince as I bend down to slide on a pair of pants. Being careful to not tear my stitches, I fumble through, pulling a Henley over my head and eventually working my arms into the sleeves.

"Seriously?" Tristan scoffs from the doorway. "What the fuck are you doing?"

"Something that needs to be done."

Something that should've already been done.

"You are a stubborn fuck."

"I need to go see Rory," I half-lie.

I'll get there eventually.

"You aren't going by yourself," Quinn grumbles as Tristan helps me down the stairs. "Someone is going with you."

"You're *all* fucking coming with me."

"I'll drive." Finn jingles the car keys in his hand.

Finn drives us all toward New York General, where I've heard Rory is making a remarkable recovery. He pulls off the FDR a few exits too soon, which surprisingly doesn't draw anyone's attention until we pull to a stop.

"What are you doing?" Quinn questions as I open her door and help her from the car.

"Something I should've done fifteen years ago," I slip my fingers into hers and walk her toward Our Lady of Grace.

"Dec. I'm not dressed for this."

"Quinn O'Brien, you could be wearing a fucking bin bag, and I wouldn't care. I am not waiting another fucking minute to marry you." Cupping her face, I pull her lips up to mine and kiss her. The type of kiss I have gone days too long without. I claim her mouth and lose myself in her until she's whimpering into my mouth.

"Now, are you going to get your arse inside that church and become my wife? Or do I need to have Finn throw your ass over his shoulder and carry you inside?"

"I guess we're going inside." She smiles as she squeezes my hand.

"Fuck yes! Let's get fucking married!" Finn shouts.

"Uncle Finn," Fiona chastises, rolling her eyes.

"Shit. Sorry, peanut. Uncle Finn forgot we don't say that."

We all laugh as we walk into the church. Flowers from our day gone wrong still hang from the ends of the pews, just as beautiful as it was four days ago. Father O'Flaherty stands at the altar, waiting for us.

"Did you?" Quinn huffs as I walk with her toward him, arm in arm.

"They did." I gesture at Finn and Tristan.

Quinn scoffs, "Finn got Father O'Flaherty to perform a last-minute Tuesday morning wedding for a couple dressed in sweatpants?"

"Let's just say I'm not allowed to miss a weekly confessional and leave it at that, okay?"

As always, I don't want to ask...

Father O'Flaherty pronounces from the altar as Quinn and I stand before him. I'm so lost in Quinn's eyes and the fact that she is finally becoming my wife that I barely hear him.

"I promise to love and cherish you all the days of my life." Quinn slides the platinum band around my finger as she speaks. "To love you with my whole heart, the way that I have loved you my entire life."

"*Mo Chéadsearc.*" I slide the platinum band around her finger until it presses against the princess-cut diamond ring nestled at the base. "I plan to spend every day with you, making up for the time that we have lost. I want to build a life with you that brings you unmeasurable happiness and love."

Tears trickle down her cheeks as I give my vows to her. I wipe one away with the pad of my thumb, only to realize that tears of my own are forming in my eyes.

"You are my first love, and you'll be my last." Quinn reaches up to swipe her finger over my cheek. "I promise to love and cherish you all the days of my life and in every lifetime that follows."

My lips are on hers before Father O'Flaherty finishes saying, "You may now kiss the bride."

I have kissed Quinn O'Brien thousands of times before, but I could not wait a second longer to kiss Quinn *Evans*. To kiss my wife.

EPILOGUE

QUINN

A little over two months later...

Declan and I have been sitting on the patio talking and listening to the water lap at the beach behind our home since putting Fiona to bed a little over an hour ago. It's one of our favorite places to unwind together.

"It's getting late, and I think it's time for bed, *mo chéadsearc*," Declan declares as he stands from his seat and takes my hand. He helps me to my feet, and I lace my fingers between his as he leads me into the house and upstairs.

Walking into our bedroom, Declan roughly pulls me into him and crashes his lips against mine. His tongue plunges into my mouth and he kisses me needily. He pulls back, leaving me wanting more as I struggle to catch my breath.

"Are you going to be a good girl for me tonight?" he asks, pulling my sweater dress over my head.

"Yes, Sir." I breathlessly exhale, unable to contain my excitement.

He walks me to the bed, kissing along the back of my neck and rubbing over the swell of my breasts. "Be a good girl and bend over," Declan commands. I bend at the waist, over the edge of the bed as his fingers run the length of my spine, until my stomach is pressed to the mattress. Reaching my panties, he hooks his fingers under them and pulls them down my thighs as he kneels behind me.

Lifting my foot to slip it from the panties, he widens my stance. His hands dust up and down my legs, working higher with every swipe until they brush against my pussy. "Already wet for me," he groans, sliding a finger along my slit. He teasingly rubs it from clit to entrance, spreading my arousal through my pussy.

Firmly gripping both my ass cheeks, Declan buries his face in my pussy from behind. *I fucking love when he eats me like this.* He licks and sucks at me as I grind my hips on his face. "You're being a naughty girl," he groans against me. "So naughty as you ride my face, trying to come."

I don't stop. *I can't.*

"Show me how badly you need it," he demands, slipping a single finger into my cunt. "Come on my face and I'll stretch you with my cock."

With his tongue on my clit and his finger thrusting into my cunt, I ride his face needily trying to reach my release. "More," I beg, and he sucks my clit into his mouth throwing me over the edge. He keeps sucking as I come, not stopping until my thighs are trembling and I'm fisting the bedsheets as I come twice more against his face.

"Thank you, Sir," I pant my appreciation against the mattress.

Declan rolls me onto my back as he rises to his feet, quickly shedding his pants. Gripping his shirt at the nape of the neck, he pulls it over his head and tosses it to the floor. My eyes roll over his chest and stomach, the scars from the three recent bullet wounds still bright pink. All a vivid display of just how much he is willing to sacrifice for me. *For our life together.*

He fists the base of the cock and slams it into me, stretching me as he promised. Hooking my legs around his hips, he holds my thighs and uses them as leverage to fuck me harder. He pants through his thrusts, "Every time I slide inside of you, all I can think about is putting my baby in you."

"Yes," I cry out as another orgasm fires through my body. "Please, Sir."

"You know. I can't fucking say no to you." He confides, increasing his pace and fucking me hard. I lift my hips, driving myself harder onto his cock with every increasingly demanding thrust. His cock grows more rigid, as he approaches his release, and it grinds against my walls forcing another orgasm from me. My pussy spasms around him and it's his undoing.

He comes with a roar, his cock twitching as he fills me. Catching his breath, he whispers, "I can't wait until I finally fuck our baby into you."

Sliding his hands up my thighs and onto my stomach, I smile up at him and share the secret I've been holding since this afternoon. "You already have, Sir."

ACKNOWLEDGMENTS

First, I would like to thank The Brat Pack. I cannot thank you enough for your belief in me and your unwavering support. You are all amazing authors, and wish each of you the greatest of success. I love you all!

Thank you to my alpha team for putting up with my absolute chaos.

As always, thank you to my husband. Quinn was wrong... Sometimes you do meet your soul-mate when you're ten. Or in our case, five. I love you with my whole heart, until my last breath.

And finally, but most definitely not least, thank you to Katie—the unsung hero behind BOUND—for pats on the head and giving me a 'good girl' praises following 3am writing sessions when I needed it most. There are not enough words for me (or Cheryl 😊) to say 'thank you.'

ALSO BY J.L. QUICK

THE MEN OF CLUB TRISKELION SERIES

- Owned
- Primal (Coming December 2024)
- Master (Coming February 2025)
- Shared (Coming April 2025)
- Daddy (Coming May 2025)

THE SAVAGELY DEPRAVED SERIES

- Dark Devils
- Family Ties
- Wicked Love
- Brutal Bond

THE BOTTICELLI BROTHERHOOD SERIES

- Sold to the Syndicate
- Capo Dei Capi's Daughter
- Indebted to the Enemy
- Falling for the Mafia Dom

THE MARCANO MOGULS SERIES

- Tryst
- Crave
- Intern
- Savage

FOLLOW ME

Join my Facebook group, J.L. Quick's Good Little Readers, to get first glimpses at covers, works in progress, chapter teasers of new releases, and more!

Use the QR to follow me on Instagram or TikTok, check out my online store for swag and signed books, and even join my newsletter!